IN AN ARID LAND

IN AN
ARID
LAND

THIRTEEN STORIES OF TEXAS

Paul Scott Malone

Texas Christian University Press
Fort Worth

Acknowledgements
"Bringing Joboy Back" first appeared in *American Fiction 88;* "Prize Rope" in *New Growth 2: Contemporary Short Stories by Texas Writers;* "The Lost Earring" in *New Virginia Review;* "The Sulfur-Colored Stone" in *Writers' Forum;* "Floundering" in *Descant;* "The Unyielding Silence" in *Southern Humanities Review;* "Mother's Thimbles" in *Writers' Forum;* "A Minor Disturbance" in *Other Voices;* "The Pier, The Porch, The Pearly Gates" in *Pembroke Magazine;* "The Wondrous Nature of Repentance" in *Concho River Review;* and "In an Arid Land" in *Black Warrior Review.*

I wish to thank the editors of these publications, Alexander Blackburn in particular, for their faith and encouragement. I also wish to thank the National Endowment for the Arts, the Society of Southwestern Authors and the University of Arizona's Program in Creative Writing for their generous support.

Library of Congress Cataloging-in-Publication Data
Malone, Paul Scott
In an arid land : thirteen stories of Texas / by Paul Scott
Malone.
p. cm.
ISBN 0-87565-140-2
1. Texas—Fiction. I. Title
PS3563.A432464I5 1995
813'.54—dc20

94-16972
CIP

1 2 3 4 5 6 7 8 9 10
Cover and text designed by Barbara Whitehead

For Cheryl

CONTENTS

PRIZE
ROPE

We're fixing up a majestic breakfast for our first morning. In my
old black skillet, on my green Coleman stove, sitting on
green metal legs above a little sand dune, nine patties of
Jimmy Dean's HOT sausage are sizzling. The sausage is my
job. I study it closely, turn each patty with the long blade
on my Swiss Army knife, sniff the wonderful greasy odor,
take a sip of my screwdriver in a plastic cup. Then I glance
up looking for Eddie.

I find him out in the surf, still in its morning calm. He's
fishing again, his big head and his long black rod silhouet-
ted against that monster sunrise. He casts, turns his body
to battle a low wave, reels in his bait like some machine.
Eddie doesn't much care for fishing; he's doing it because
that's what men do when they go to the beach, and
because he's heartbroken.

"What's on his mind?" Ed Senior wants to know, com-

ing up behind me. "I don't think he slept at all and he
hasn't spoken a word since we got up, just a grunt now and
then, like an animal."

"Squaw problems," I say.

"That's what I figured," he says.

"So what's new, huh?"

"Dern women," says Ed Senior and he snorts a laugh to
show he's joking; he doesn't know the facts of the matter. I
know the facts and I know it's not Marcia's fault that
Eddie's heartbroken; this is No-Fault Heartbreak, you
might say. She changed, he changed, they changed, an old
American story; and I happen to know she's in Albuquerque this week looking for a place to live.

We stand there worrying, wearing nothing but swim
trunks, wriggling our toes in the sand, me with my knife,
him with his Dutch oven full of biscuits, staring out to sea
like wives of old. Eddie's my best friend, has been most of
my life, and he's Ed Senior's only son. We've come here, to
this lonely stretch of beach, because Eddie wanted us to.
An empty house is a mean companion. So here we are,
three white guys loose upon the earth.

"Dern women," the Old One says again, grinning at me
as he turns away. He goes back to his fire pit, pokes the
coals with a stick and replaces the Dutch oven on the
blackened grate. The biscuits, the coffee, the fried potatoes with onions and some kind of private seasoning he
brought along—these are Ed Senior's jobs, and he knows
what he's doing. The eggs are Eddie's job.

"Is it time yet?"

"Pretty close," he says. "Better call him in."

We both look out to sea. Eddie casts again, reels it in
like he's in a bad hurry, with an awkward but furious kind
of precision, like it's a chore he's got to get through but
never will.

It's unlikely he'll catch anything; we all know this. There's a fat old noisy dredge as big as a destroyer working in the shrimp boat channel just down the island from us and it's pumping the sludge over the jetties into the Gulf. Just our luck. The water all around is gray and gritty, the fish gone elsewhere.

I turn the sausage for the last time, slice off a juicy bite to be sure it's done, put down my knife and then I trudge through the sand to the water. I stand in the water, staring at Eddie, just watching him, still silent, until he turns and sees me.

∼

After breakfast Ed Senior mixes up a new round of screwdrivers. He squeezes a lime wedge into each red cup and tells us it's his own personal recipe. We grin like conspirators, touch cups in a toast and then sit in folding chairs beneath the shelter we have erected with a blue plastic tarp and four crooked poles of driftwood. Ed Senior slaps Eddie's knee and shows an enormous smile to be uplifting. He says, "Boys, this is the life, ain't it?"

The tarp flaps and complains overhead. We sip our drinks, smoke cigarettes we wouldn't smoke back in the city, breathe in the salty air, gaze at the roaring Gulf. Already it's ninety degrees and we're sweating, our pale bodies suffering.

It's an elaborate camp we have made. Our huge rented tent snaps and grumbles in the anxious breeze. Inside is all our personal gear, knapsacks and satchels and gimme caps, books that won't get read, two sleeping bags, Ed Senior's aluminum cot, a *Playboy* magazine, a .357 Ruger automatic, our wallets full of money and credit cards and fishing licenses purchased at a bait shop yesterday, along with tiny photos of loved ones. Round about are ice chests and old trunks, jugs of fresh water and big red gasoline cans, pairs of sneakers and tackle boxes already settling into the sand. A second spare tire, which the park rangers suggested we bring along when Eddie called last week, serves as the bar; it is covered with leaning liquor bottles and even, as a sort of joke by Ed Senior which we the young ones don't get, a metal martini mixer and a squat round decanter of expensive liqueur.

"Grace and style, boys," he explained when he emptied the "liquor store," one of the trunks, while we were setting up camp.

To put it straight, we overloaded. The roof of Eddie's big Jeep was weighted down so cruelly on our drive down here that the ceiling liner touched my head in the backseat. Better to have than to have not was our motto in packing. We are sixty-three miles from civilization. We are a long way from home. We are without supervision. This is how he wanted it; he wanted Remote. He has owned the Jeep for two years, put 64,000 miles on it, and yesterday, grinding through the deep soft sand in our search for Remote, was only the third time he has used the four-wheel drive.

Eddie rises, gulps the rest of his drink and without a word to either of us he picks up his rod and his bait can and then he walks like a man with a mission straight into the water.

∼

We fish for a while, catch nothing, but it feels good being in the warm surf, which is up now and fighting us. We're on the first sandbar. The water is groin deep. Ed Senior and I are working the trench between us and the beach. Eddie's still casting out, into the oncoming waves. He reaches way back with his brand-new surf rig and heaves with all his might, sending the sinker and the shrimp on its hook into a tremendous arc that ends with a tiny splash out among the breakers. Each time he looks somehow disappointed, as if he's trying to hit Florida or the Gulf Stream with every toss and intends to keep at it until he does.

Soon Ed Senior tires of the fight. I can see it in his drooping red face, his weary gray hair. He waves at me, points to the camp and smiles before he wades through the trench to the beach. He dries himself, changes into some baggy plaid shorts and a polo shirt, and I see him disappear into the tent for a nap.

Another hour of nothing. Now I'm tired too and I can feel the sting of the sun on my white-boy shoulders. Eddie the Machine is still working, casting out and reeling in, casting out and reeling in. I make my way down the sandbar to him, and he actually flinches and jumps when he senses me there beside him. He looks at me like I'm a Hammerhead come to eat him.

"Let's go in," I yell over the roar.

He shakes his head no, indicates with a nod that I should go ahead though if I want to. He reels in, turns to toss again and it's then that I notice there's no bait on his hook—nothing but curved steel. With that same look in his face he heaves and sends his naked hook flying toward Florida.

I yell, "Hey, man, they've stolen your bait."

Eddie glances at me with those cool blue eyes in his reddening face and he shrugs his reddening shoulders as if it doesn't matter, and he starts reeling in again. So I leave him there and slog it to the beach. In camp I find one of his tee shirts flapping from a pole of the shelter.

On the front of the tee shirt, in faded blue letters above and below a faded blue stencil of a big Texas gobbler, it says, *Thanksgiving Day Turkey Trot — A Marathon for Health — Greater Houston Heart Association.* I remember that day. I remember a photograph of Eddie and Marcia, their faces worn out and drained of color but happy, their dark hair stringy and wild under their sweatbands, his hammy arm across her shoulders, and each of them wearing a Turkey Trot tee shirt. They're looking right into the camera and their eyes are the Lights of Expectation. Also in the picture are his mom and Ed Senior, who'd come in to town for the occasion, beaming like proud parents should. I took that picture, though I hadn't run in the race, to celebrate his return from the brink. He was healthy again after two years of struggling with it — the crud in his veins, the goo in his lungs, those murderous habits — and we were crazy with joy and love for what he'd done.

Back into the waves I go, carrying the tee shirt on a mission of mercy, and when I get to him I holler, "Hey, better put this on, you're roasting." He smiles at me and nods his head in thanks. I take his rod while he slips the shirt on and I very quickly bait his hook with a shrimp out of my own can.

He smiles again, nods again, takes the rod from me, turns, heaves, trying once again for Florida.

~

About mid-afternoon Ed Senior emerges from the tent squinting and blinking in the blinding glare of sun and sand.

"Good God, Matt, is he still at it?"

"Yessir," I say.

"Has he caught anything?"

"Not that I've noticed."

We glance at each other with looks of wonder and concern, and then sit under the sagging shelter drinking beers.

We sit there for quite a while, saying little, just watching Eddie out in the surf, the flight of an occasional pelican, a sand crab scampering about. The tarp above us is whooshing like a flag now.

Ed Senior is restless after his nap. He fidgets in his chair, scans the beach looking for entertainment. All of a sudden he says, "Hey, let's go do some scavenging, want to?"

"Well sure. Sounds fine with me."

"Wonder if he'll come along?" he says, looking out at Eddie.

"He's got to be tired."

"Gotta be."

"We'll coax him out with beer."

We take six cans from an ice chest and with two of them raised high I struggle through the water to the sandbar while Ed Senior starts the Jeep and drives down to the water's edge to wait. It's a reluctant Eddie who follows me out. He gets in the back seat and the Old One drives us up the beach in the direction we came from yesterday. The tide is out and so Ed Senior guns up the Jeep, races along the wet hard pack, splashing through pockets of water, and we're all grinning over it like riders on a roller coaster. Soon we're at the part of the island where the junk, the jetsam and flotsam, the debris, the detritus — whatever you want to call it — is the worst, the deepest, the ugliest.

It's a depressing sight — "like the Aftermath," as Eddie put it yesterday when we ground our way through here — but heartening, too, to scavengers like us. In the soft sand between the tide line and the high grassy dunes is all the stuff of modern life. Plastic laundry hampers, plastic milk crates, plastic jugs, half submerged in the sand. Huge chunks of lumber with rusty nails protruding dangerously.

Hypodermic needles, little brown bottles, big green bottles, faded beer cans, lengths of oceangoing rope. Gifts from Mexico, New Jersey, Europe and all the ships at sea.

We wander through it, watching where we step, picking up this, picking up that, tossing it down. Soon we settle on rope as our objective — no telling what you might use it for. We drive a ways, spot a telltale yellow piece poking out of the sand, stop, get out, pull on it, and twenty feet surface in a long circular line. Two hours we stalk the beach, going five, maybe six miles, until there are two filthy laundry baskets full of coiled, stinking rope in the back of the Jeep. The Prize Piece is perhaps two inches in diameter, perhaps thirty feet long, with impressive loops woven into both ends. Eddie, smiling, says he'll use it as a clothesline, "or maybe to hang myself when the time comes."

Now we are disgusted with scavenging, hot and stinking and exhausted, and headed back to camp. Eddie's driving. He's going fast, right at the water's edge — the roller coaster again, only faster, more erratic — up and down off low dunes, splashing through cuts in the beach at forty, fifty, sixty miles an hour. We're whizzing along, enjoying the cool breeze, the thrill.

Eddie, grinning ferociously, says, loud over the wind noise, "About time this Jeep started to look and act like a Jeep," and he takes us bounding over a little ridge. "Look at this," he says, pointing to a streak of beach tar on the pretty gray dashboard. "Now that's the way it ought to look." He guns it up, grins all around, his hair blowing, eyes bright. "Watch this," he says and this time all four tires come off the ground.

"Wahoo," I holler, caught up in the moment, his moment.

But I can tell Ed Senior is worried. The Old One is

hanging on and frowning now with doubt. He wants to say
something but won't, wants to be fatherly but can't. Eddie
knows this. He glances over, returns his father's frown, and
without warning he turns the Jeep into the surf, sending
up spray like a motorboat, soaking us all, and then, stamping his foot on the brake pedal, he takes us to a rough tilt-
ing stop. The Jeep rocks up painfully on its side and hangs
there for a tense moment before settling itself like a great
wounded beast. Eddie smiles and looks around.

"Holy cow, boy, you trying to kill us?" says Ed Senior,
and he lets out a nervous laugh. "This ain't a Pershing
tank, you know."

Eddie opens his door and gets out. He runs, leaping
through the waves, and dives in. Ed Senior and I sit there
in the sweltering Jeep, wondering what he's doing.

He emerges, splashes back in, comes right up to the
Jeep and leans his big head inside the window, dripping
water.

"Y'all go ahead," he says, panting, his face blazing red.
"I'll see you in a little while."

"We can wait," says Ed Senior. "Whatever you're doing."

"Naw, go on, I'm collecting sea shells."

"Sea shells!" says the Old One. "What for?"

Eddie backs away into the water, panting and smiling
oddly, bends at the waist like a runner to catch his breath,
and looks at our wondering faces through the window.

"Because Marcia likes sea shells," he says.

He turns, runs away, jumping through the waves like a
big old crazy dog, stretches out his body and dives in
again.

~

The sunset's full above the dunes by the time Eddie
appears in camp. Ed Senior, a martini in his hand, com-

plete with olives, is moving fretfully around the fire pit.
He has supper well under way — not the broiled snapper
we'd planned on, but steaks and baked potatoes and even
sweet corn, a fine meal.

"About goddamn time you showed up," he says to Eddie
in a lilting, teasing voice. "Where're your sea shells?"

It's true; he walked in empty handed.

Giving the Old One a mean glare for bringing it up,
Eddie says, "I'm not hungry, don't fix me anything," and
Ed Senior returns the glare, his mouth hanging open in
exaggerated shock.

"But you gotta make the salad, I'm no good with salad."

"I don't want anything, I tell you."

"Ah, for crying out loud," says Ed Senior. "You can't go
without eating, son, you haven't had a bite since breakfast."

"I can go without anything I damn well want to go
without," he says, and we're both a little hurt by his tone.
We shuffle around in the sand, looking away, glancing
back. Eddie seems to regret it but he's not apologizing. In
haste he finds his rod and his bait can and he marches out
to sea. He's lucky. The moon, about two slivers shy of full,
is already up out there, hanging above the horizon like a
great white eye giving off a big light.

"Well, I'll say this," the Old One grumbles after a long
while. "If determination could feed the world, ole Eddie'd
be the breadbasket, wouldn't he? Or maybe the fishing net."

"He'll get over it," I say, thinking hard. "I guess I did."

We glance at each other in the fading sunset, knowing
I'm lying in the service of friendship, knowing these are not
the facts of the matter, both of us wishing I hadn't said it.

"Let's eat," he mutters, turning toward the fire pit, and
we are very quiet with each other all through the meal.

～

It's late now. The big eye of the moon has crawled well up into the starry sky, its bright light intruding on our privacy, even here, in Remote, Texas. Ed Senior and I have long since had our feast of steak and potatoes, long since concluded that we should leave Eddie's meal warming in the Dutch oven above the coals, long since passed between us the squat round decanter of expensive liqueur that tasted of orange peels and sugar water, long since given up our inebriated talk of nothing (that worthless drowsy kind of talk that always follows the lowering of the lantern's flame when the newly arrived gloom of night involves you in its promise of rest), long since had our sighs and our yawns and let our heads nod, long since offered our good-nights.

The Old One is in the tent, snoring. From my folding chair I can hear him over the night sounds of the surf, and it is somehow endearing to me and comforting.

"Better keep an eye on him," he mumbled before he went to bed, which is what I have done more or less, dozing and waking and watching. Long after midnight and he's still out there, on the first sandbar, casting out and reeling in, casting out and reeling in, trying to hit Florida, a dark irregularity in the triangular gloss of reflected moonlight, a human chink in a piece of finely wrought silver made beautiful by the imperfection.

At last I rouse myself and carry my folding chair out to the very edge of the water. I smoke cigarettes I shouldn't smoke, drink a beer I shouldn't drink, find the Big Dipper, imagine for a while, and then, growing bored with its simple design, I wish I were a smarter man who knew the positions and configurations of other constellations so that I could find them, too, and imagine even more. Off in the distance, beyond the jetties, the fat old dredge in the channel shines like a small city, its red and white lights

speaking of other humans hereabout, rough working guys
doing their jobs all through the night, reminding me that
we are never, in the modern world, as remote as we'd like
to think.

I am, on the whole, terrified of dark water. There are
wily sharks out there and jellyfish and stingrays and
killer currents and no telling what else, and I am
amazed, still, that my friend does not share this terror.
Friendship, like love, I think, is one of the grand mysteries. Who knows what brings strangers together and
drives comrades apart? Living with the mystery takes
courage, I know, the courage to stand in dark water and
to cast your line toward Florida, the courage to hope
that, in spite of yourself, ignoring the odds, you just
might catch something.

Back in camp I take our Prize Rope out of the Jeep and
then I fumble around until I find my rod and my bait
can. Dragging the rope, I walk out into the water until
it's lapping at my thighs. A sneaky chill wriggles across
my back and I have to stop. The trench is just before me,
deep and hidden and fearful, and it takes me a moment
to plunge in. When I do I go ahead quickly, kicking
through the water, trailing the heavy rope behind, until
I'm up safely on the sandbar and making my way toward
Eddie.

When I'm close enough to hear, he calls out above the
waves, "Been wondering when you'd show up." His voice
is eerie-sounding, louder now and more distinct, out here
in the watery void.

"Well I've never much cared for bathing with sharks."

I can see him smile in the moonlight, his teeth shining
like phosphorescent gems. He's glad to see me, and I'm
glad I came.

"What's that?" he says, noticing the rope.

"This, my friend, is our lifeline," I say. "Here, put this loop around your waist."

At first he laughs, says, "What?!" but when he sees I'm serious he does what he's told. We take turns holding our gear as the other one slips the rope over his head and slithers into it, a slow clumsy business. It's a heavy weight, but the water buoys the rope somewhat and when it's done I feel better.

"Why don't you take over for a while, I'm tired out."

"Have you caught anything?"

"Naw," he says. "Will though, I've had nibbles."

I dig into my can and pull out a shrimp, bait my hook, prick my finger in the process and worry that I'm bleeding, calling the sharks in for dinner. I cast out, let the sinker settle to the bottom, the way it ought to be done. My plan is to do it right, thinking if I catch something for him maybe he'll give it up, get some rest. Slowly I reel in, letting it settle, dragging it in, but I come up with nothing. So I cast out and try again.

As if it's the next line in a long conversation, he says, "You know what she told me the day she left for Albuquerque?" and he looks at me as if this is significant, something I need to know. "She said — I can still hear her voice like she was standing right there where you are — she said, 'It is possible I will miss you when I leave.'"

We give off looks full of injury and confusion, but I don't know what to say to him, don't know what to do, don't know why he told me that, so I reel in my bait and cast out again. Thinking about it, imagining his misery, I find myself reeling in without any thought of catching fish. I want to say something, I want to sound wise and brotherly, but I've never been any good at that sort of thing and when I open my mouth nothing comes out.

"It-is-*possible*," I hear him say again, emphasizing each

word, trying to understand them, I guess, dwelling on it, "I-will-*miss*-you . . ." and he pauses here, ". . . *when-I-leave*."

We are quiet for a while as the waves roll through us, holding our rods tightly in our hands, glancing at each other.

"I've been out here all day," he says. "And what I can't figure out is why anybody that once loved you, once shared everything with you, why she would ever say something like that to you." He looks over. He says, "You got any ideas?"

"No," I say, and it's the truth. I wish I did, I wish I had all kinds of ideas, but I don't and he knows I don't.

I cast out and reel it in, without method, without purpose, moving down the sandbar to get away from him since I don't want to hear any more. What good is such talk? When I'm out of hearing range, and the rope, our lifeline, is stretched to its fullest, I look back, keeping an eye on him as the Old One has asked me to. I can see his white Turkey Trot tee shirt glowing in the moonlight and his big head low against his chest and I think perhaps he is weeping. It would have been better, I think, if he hadn't said anything, hadn't mentioned Marcia's last words to him, words uttered in haste and anger and meant to hurt him, which they did, and then did again. But heartbreak is like that, I know.

I tug on the rope, gently, rhythmically, so he won't know it's not the waves doing the tugging, just enough to draw him off balance and away from his thoughts, and he seems to come out of the spell. Presently he lifts his rod and he turns and he heaves his sinker out into the dark churning waves, and, because this is why I have come, I do the same, and then we both reel in, quite deliberately, keeping our eyes on some invisible spot out there, and this goes on and on, on and on for a long time; we cast out and reel in, cast out and reel in, catching nothing, as the sharks and the stingrays and the jellyfish swim menacingly around us, as the killer currents conspire against us, as the moon ducks its big white eye below the dunes behind us, all through the blind mysterious hours, while the Prize Rope tugs at our waists, keeping us close, until, with the first pale sheen of sunrise, we can see once again just where we are, see once again the danger we have passed through together.

THE
LOST
EARRING

Angelica wakes in the night and in the blue milky sheen of the moon's thin rays she sees a strange luminescent figure in the room with her. At first she is frightened; at first she reaches up a hand to protect herself. But then the common sense of the conscious mind says *No no, it is only Miguel come to me for comfort after a bad dream.*

He waits at the foot of the bed, small as his father was small, erect and stern and ghostly. His nightshirt with the cartoon fighting turtles on the front glows in the eerie moonlight. His eyes are dark sockets, his nose sharp as a jagged stone. And for a moment then he is the image and the essence of his father come to speak to her, come to explain himself, come to advise her perhaps. She has hundreds of questions, he must have all kinds of stories to tell of his adventures. But again the common sense of the conscious mind overrules longing, and again she sees it is only her son standing there.

She says, "What is it, Miguel, what is wrong?"

He says nothing; he only stares. A long moment passes before he moves: around the footboard and up onto the bed in one fluid motion, swift and graceful. He buries his head in the hollow between arm and breast and clamps a hand on her body as if to keep her from floating away.

"What scared you? What has happened? Is Gabe all right?"

He is slow to answer; what he has to say will startle and alarm and even frighten again.

"What was it, sweetheart, a dream?"

"No," he says, mumbling into the soft hollow of his mother's body. "No, it was you. You were talking again."

"Oh, I see. And what did I say?"

"You said, 'Hold me. . . .'"

"That's all?"

"The rest I couldn't listen to."

She imagines her voice slipping out the door cracks and through the walls to his small room and creeping up to his small bed and entering his small ears and she knows in that instant the same panic he must have felt. She apologizes and coos to him, tells him it's all right now, he can sleep here in her big bed and if she speaks out again he will know it is nothing.

"Just wake me up. Say 'hush, Mama, hush!' It is nothing, just something that happens sometimes."

He seems relieved; his breathing calms.

Neither of them sleeps again.

⌒

When Jorge disappeared in a plane crash (deep in the mountains of Venezuela where he had gone to write a profile of a promising minor-league ballplayer) Angelica saw it for a while as a kind of death for herself as well, a spiritual death, as if a vital part of her had been cut out and sent flying into Purgatory. She hated everything and everybody, for what is the loss of the beloved if not the loss of the faculty to love?

They had been together so long, for one thing — eighteen years. Their mature lives were completely tangled up together, always, like two snakes in a cage. And there were the boys — Miguel, nine, Gabriel, six. It had not been easy, those years, with the waiting, the trying (she conceived with difficulty) and the difficult births. And so little money then for shoes, for toys, for even the necessities some months, though toward the end they had sensed a change. A nest egg in the bank, at last a new car, talk of buying a house. At thirty-nine her life had just begun to assume a concrete form, a heft and weight of its own, a settled feeling that would have carried her well into old age.

She took to her bed. She existed only in the internal passageways, the internal landscapes of grief and loneliness. The grandmothers, both in far distant cities, each kept one of the boys during that time of chaos. Then one day her mother appeared. *Bastante es bastante, Angelica. Take a hold now. You are a woman with responsibilities. Do you think you are the first woman to lose her husband?* All of this in the shrill chastising voice of a mother's frustration and wisdom. Her own husband, Angelica's father, had been a drunk who died on a dusty street; she had raised four children alone and had *not* raised them to be weaklings. *Get up from there and get on with it.*

She did. They were understanding at the university where she works as the Minority Recruitment Officer. They like her, respect her; they wanted her back. And the boys came home. But she couldn't stay anymore in the little house on Laredo Street where Jorge's voice even now sounded in her memories. So she found another, same rent but even nicer, larger, with two small rooms upstairs for the boys and her own room below. It was here, she told herself, that she would start her life over.

~

Angelica goes to her new landlady's house to get the key and pay the rent. The landlady is the daughter of the old man whose house she is taking now, now that his wife is dead and he can no longer tend to his affairs. He lives with the daughter in a fine old place just a few blocks from the house Angelica is renting.

He is sitting at the kitchen table when Angelica arrives. The daughter, a slim woman with graying hair, is nervous but friendly. She has never been a landlady before, never had an old one to care for, and she is uncertain just how to go about it.

The *viejito* is very old. He sits at the table with his hands folded in his lap. He wears baggy trousers and a baggy shirt; his feet are bare. His head is bald but for thin silvery patches on the sides above his long purple ears, and the skin is splotched. His face is thin, the cheeks sunken, the chin gray with days' old stubble, but his eyes are brilliant and blue.

He looks at Angelica fiercely, directly, almost aggressively with those brilliant blue eyes, as if she is an interloper or a loved one who has disappointed. In fact he stares at her quite rudely until the daughter says, "Papa? Papa!" in a loud voice. "Papa, don't be so rude, don't stare at our guest."

His eyes blink but his gaze does not shift or change.

"He hasn't been quite the same since Mother died," the daughter says to Angelica. "They were together forty-seven years, you see, and he remembers too well at times, the old days, and he forgets too well sometimes too — isn't that right, Papa?"

"Yes!" the old man says to quiet his daughter's prattle and then suddenly he changes, he softens. Looking softly at Angelica, he asks, "Did you ever find that earring you lost in the bedroom, the pearl I gave you as a wedding present?"

He smiles now as if speaking in fondness — his blue eyes dance a bit; there is something playful and lusty and familiar in them — and he tilts his head awaiting an answer. It is all incredible and disquieting to Angelica, this question, this coincidence. Not long ago she did indeed lose an earring, much cherished, and she couldn't find it when packing to move. She knows though; she knows he is not truly speaking to her but to that other woman whose house and bedroom he shared all those years.

"Papa," says the daughter in her embarrassment, touching his arm, "this is not Mama, this is Angelica," and yet the old man waits and smiles expecting an answer.

Angelica smiles too now and says, because he wants her to be the woman he thinks she is, "No, I didn't find it. It's still lost, there in the bedroom somewhere."

He is very pleased by her answer. His smile changes, deepens to one of regret and compassion and resignation to the unknown parts of life, the elusive ways of small hidden things. There is a touch of pity too, and even more, something else.

"So then," he says with a kind of masculine decisiveness. "I'll have to have a look later. My eyes are better than yours."

"Yes," she says. "They always have been."

"Hah! That's true, I got the eyes, you got the

ears — and the bazoobs," he says, eyes blazing and playful, tongue showing lewdly between his teeth, and without a hint of shame he cups his hands and moves them vaguely before his chest.

"You should know," says Angelica in a lilting, teasing voice, almost laughing now at their game.

The old man rolls his eyes and tosses his head — he is nearly ecstatic now with joy and delight — and then he flops back in his chair. He lets out one loud laugh.

The daughter is mystified and a bit mortified by this conversation between her father and this stranger. She glances at Angelica with a look that says, *Don't encourage him, please.*

"He gets confused at times," she says. Then: "Papa? Papa, would you like to take a walk?" Then: "He likes to walk through the neighborhood. Everyone knows him. They understand. He even goes back to the old house at times for a look, just a look."

"I see," says Angelica. And then to the old man: "Stop in anytime, Mr. Morris, we'd love to have you."

He seems to comprehend this, to be of this world again, and he eyes her again in that direct, almost aggressive way of his.

The daughter says, "Papa? Well yes, why don't you take a walk. But you'll have to put your shoes on, Papa, and your hat."

Angelica writes out a check as the daughter gets him up and helps him prepare. She guides him out the door and sends him down the drive to the sidewalk. Back inside she apologizes for her father, makes excuses for his age and the loss of his mind.

"You must look familiar to him," the daughter says. "Mother had black hair too, and wore glasses."

Angelica takes the key to her new house and leaves.

The old man, tall but stooped under his floppy hat, his trousers dragging the pavement of the sidewalk, his cane tapping, is halfway down the block when she drives by. She waves but he does not look up.

~

It's late October now and the leaves are changing. The town is canopied in bright shades of yellow and red. The air is crisp, easy to inhale. On the front doors of the houses in the neighborhood hang plastic images of jack-o-lanterns, skeletons, witches. In the weeks since Angelica and the boys moved in to the house life has passed peacefully and well. They have settled in, made a home with their things around them and their routines re-established. But today something is wrong, something is up.

The boys sense it as a danger. She was late to pick them up at the day care, spanked Gabe over nothing and in the car there is an ominous silence. By the time they reach the house the boys are frightened of her mood and go to their rooms to play alone.

She believes she can trace what is wrong, trace it to its origins. For lunch that day she went with several colleagues to the Union. There were six of them, four women and two men. They talked shop, complained and commiserated. It was pleasant and relaxing and they were all cheerful when they got up to leave.

But one of them, a man named Alfred who works in Admissions, a nice man, heavyset and bearded, with curly graying hair and a tiny, tiny nose, a gentle man — Alfred asked her to wait a moment, he wanted to speak to her. The others grinned among themselves and as they were leaving they glanced back with knowing eyes.

Alfred, who has always been rather formal with her, said he had been meaning to speak to her for several weeks but had wanted to avoid seeming "pushy and unfair to Jorge." He wanted to know if she would "consent," it is the very word he used, to his asking her out to dinner. He thought enough time had passed and there was no point in their both being alone so often. Alfred is divorced and has a daughter he sees on weekends. He is known as a good man, an honorable man, a conscientious man, even if he is heavyset and slow of speech and just slightly on the ugly side. She has known him for many years now and has always liked him.

This, however . . . this she has not expected. She has not yet even considered seeing other men. It has been so long, and even in her youth she dated very little. She and Jorge never really "dated" at all in the common way; they were acquaintances and then lovers and then married in a matter of months. And what would she talk about with some other man, even Alfred Dunn? There is nothing to her but Jorge and the boys and her work, and he knows all about her work. No, she was not ready, is not ready, doesn't even want to be ready. Besides, she has too much to do, to think about, to be going out nights.

So she said to Alfred, "Thank you but I couldn't, not yet."

"I see," said Alfred in his gentle way. "I understand."

He looked so dejected! But why? This is Angelica, only Angelica. There are plenty of others, ask them. But then, for reasons she could not fathom, she said, "Well, all right, I'll tell you what, let me think about it. Maybe."

"Oh yes, good," he said, bright and hopeful. "You really should get out more. You shouldn't sit in that house and brood."

"I don't brood, Alfred."

They looked at each other through their eyeglasses and it seemed they had reached an understanding.

All day long she thought about it and then she thought about what Jorge would think of it and then she thought only of Jorge. She thought of him deeply, intensely, self-ishly. By day's end she had fashioned in her mind a model of anger and resentment toward him. *If you left me you must not have loved me and if you did not love me then you must have wanted to leave me. Isn't death, after all, simply a giving up, a getting out?*

At home, after the boys have eaten their dinner in silence and been put to bed early, she goes to her room and broods in the darkness. Her body is cold and hollow. She feels weak, too weak to make decisions, too weak even to lie down, to sleep. She doesn't want to go to din-ner with Alfred Dunn, she doesn't want to go to dinner with anybody; she wants Jorge to come home.

The moon is up again. At the window she looks out at the street, at the huge live oak in the yard. Jorge would have liked that tree. He was a great tree climber, an adventurer. It is then that she notices a dark figure on the sidewalk. She puts on her glasses and sees Mr. Morris standing there, resting against his cane. He is studying the house; he seems to be searching the windows for some-thing. She steps back into the deeper shadow of her safe place and watches.

He is like a dead man come to life, a wandering shade, the pure image of loneliness. His bald head shines in the moonlight and his clothes hang on him loosely. Now he is looking down, as if in thought. Perhaps he is lost and con-fused, can't recall the way home. An odd and disturbing notion, for he has found his way home: to this house where he lived all those years with a wife he must have loved. Here it was they raised their children and tended their gardens and slept together in this very room. She wonders if this is what he is thinking, if this is what he is remembering, and if in the vapors of his senility he is searching for the key to come inside.

Soon he turns and shuffles away, tapping the sidewalk with his cane, and once again the night is empty.

~

"When is Daddy coming home?" Gabe wants to know.

It is the weekend. They are all on the front porch, the broad deep porch that first attracts the eye when you approach the house. Miguel is playing with his turtles but he won't allow Gabe to join him and Gabe is bored and angry and frustrated. He wants Daddy to play with him, though Mama will do. But Mama is busy; she is reading reports; she has a meeting of district recruiters on Monday and she is not prepared.

"When is Daddy coming home?" he asks again, demanding and violent this time. He stalks to Angelica's chair and shakes it.

She glances at him and answers without thinking, "Never."

Now Miguel stops his playing and looks up. They are both staring at her. Never has she said *never*. Never has she so directly stated the cold simple fact of it. Still, she is surprised by their response. She thought they had accepted the fact; she thought that after so much time they would have forgotten. Now she sees, as she has not seen before, her own face in the faces of these two young ones: the eyes of doubt, the brows deep and furrowed by the mystery of it.

None of them says a word. She drops her papers to the porch and snatches Gabe into her arms; she beckons Miguel to her side; she clutches at them both. Together they send up a wail of misery as the tears course down their cheeks.

And here is Mr. Morris standing on the porch steps. The boys don't notice him but Angelica is startled by his presence. She did not see him approach; he is simply there. At first this scene must strike him as humorous — these three small people huddled together and weeping in broad public daylight. There is a hint of a smile on his dry thin lips. But as Angelica tries to recover, dabbing her tears, his face changes. The touch of pity returns, along with traces of compassion and tenderness. He steps up onto the porch. He looms above them.

The boys know now; they hear him; they turn. They see him and without any self-consciousness they grab him and hold him and weep anew against him, wiping their eyes on the canvas of his trousers. He touches their shoulders, pats them, speaks softly.

"I was just passing by," he says to Angelica.

Angelica stands, apologizes, tries to right the spilled appearance of her family. She tells the boys to leave Mr. Morris alone, he is not here to be soaked by their tears, but the old man shakes his head, flaps a hand, says, "It's okay."

"They miss their father."

"So do I sometimes," he says. "Even now after all these years I miss my old man. In the old days, he used to come here and we would sit on this very porch and pass the time. He helped me plant that tree." And then, embarrassed by his memories and his confiding, he says: "Hey, what's this?"

He has spied Miguel's toys scattered on the porch. He seems interested, willing. Miguel is thrilled by his interest. He wants to show, to tell. He flies to the end of the porch and slides into the toys. He calls over Mr. Morris. He lets Gabe explain one or two of the simpler aspects of the turtles' intricate parts and behavior. The old man sits among them. Presently the three of them are deep in maneuvers, the two young ones in combat with the old one. Angelica, baffled a bit but thankful, sits in her chair on the porch and watches. They play for a long time, with excitement and laughter, and Mr. Morris gallantly loses.

That night they have pizza for supper, they watch TV, and things are better.

~

But now comes Alfred Dunn. It is late Sunday morning when his car eases to a stop at the curb. Out he spills with a bag of donuts and *The New York Times*. Angelica meets him at the door, still in her robe. The boys are on the porch again. They know Alfred but act as if they don't; they act as if he is no one worth knowing. They glance up and go back to their playing.

"It's a nice day and I thought maybe. . . ." He holds up his gifts by way of finishing the sentence.

Angelica resents his dropping by but she invites him in anyway. She notices that he is clean and neat, dressed in new jeans, a new tee shirt, and his hair is still damp from the shower. Despite the morning mess of misplaced toys and clothing and pizza boxes on the coffee table, Alfred praises the house, tells her how lucky she was to find it. She agrees, says they like it, it suits them. He sits at the table. She puts on more coffee. They eat donuts and talk of work, of mutual friends.

Why is he here? What does he want?

"Angelica," he says suddenly, and he scoots his chair around the table to be closer to her. "Have you thought about what I asked you? If you won't consent to going out with me, maybe you would consent to my, well. . . ." He shrugs, glances around. "Well, to my just coming here, just to be together."

Now she thinks she knows why he has come. He has taken her hand. With the other, the free hand, she holds the lapels of her robe together. She is too surprised to do more, too stunned to say no, to say anything, and he must take her silence as tacit approval. He kisses her on the lips; he touches her breast; he tries to surround her with his arms.

"Come, let's go to the bedroom," he whispers.

She can't believe what is happening. It is a Sunday morning. The boys were playing quietly. She was working quietly. Everything was as it should have been and now here is Alfred Dunn — sweet Alfred Dunn, who once loaned her money, who supports her arguments in departmental meetings, who used to play softball on the same team with Jorge. Here is Alfred Dunn wanting her body, wanting her love.

The screen door slams. There is a loud stamping of little feet on the hard wooden floors. Up rises the usual: "Mom?"

Alfred jumps back. Angelica jumps to her feet. The boys are there, in the room, gazing at them in disbelief. It is a long and awful moment, frozen with shame. "Yes, Miguel, what is it?" she asks. And the disbelief vanishes. They are no longer shocked; they no longer care. At the sound of their mother's voice, so common, so feeble, she thinks, they realize that what they saw must have been an illusion. It is only Alfred, after all, and besides they are in the wrong room for such things. The boys have seen Angelica and Jorge kissing, seen them even naked, but always in the bedroom. This is the kitchen, where dinner is cooked, meals are served, arguments thrashed out. It is not for kissing.

Miguel says, coarse and direct, "He won't play right, I'm going over to Mack's house." Then Gabe makes his complaint, "He won't ever let me win," and he stomps up the stairs to his room. The screen door slams again; Miguel is gone. It is another awful moment. She is afraid he will say, *Now, we're alone, come with me.*

She finds her voice; she says, "I think you'd better go."

"Yes, of course, I'm sorry."

"Don't apologize, Alfred, just go. Please."

He leaves with heavy footsteps.

~

Midnight now and not a sound. The boys upstairs are asleep, she assumes, she hopes, in their costumes. Tomorrow, Monday, is Halloween and they couldn't wait to try on their outfits. Gabe will be a pirate and Miguel a skeleton. His costume is black with white lines showing the bones, the headpiece skull-like. Once dressed, they insisted on sleeping in their assumed identities and after a brief but furious dispute she relented. She imagines them now, curled in their separate beds up there, close and yet far away in this tainted house, and she thinks she should go up and check on them. But not tonight; she hasn't the will to move. The weekend and its afflictions have drained her of everything.

So she will remain where she is, lying in her bed as she has been lying in it for some time now. Sleep is doubtful, but there is solace here, a certain soft and giving nature that comforts more than the weary body, and there are memories that come so clearly at times she can't distinguish them as memories. The morning they bought the bed at a garage sale and cheerfully brought it home; the way the mattress sags, always has, and used to draw them together at its center; the way Jorge would sprawl across it for a few more moments of rest when she had risen for the day. This was their place, their one true haven in the world.

She hears something out in the house. A creaking door perhaps? Feet skittering across the floor? A bump against a table? She is uncertain but for this: someone is there. Must be one of the boys come down for a glass of water or some mischief.

She should go see; she should help if she can, stop the mischief if that's what it is. When Jorge was alive this was his job, his duty, to rise in the night and see what was wrong, as it was his duty to scold and reprimand, for she seldom had the strength or the courage to correct and guide at midnight.

Get up from there and get on with it, her mother's voice reminds, and again she obeys. She switches on her lamp; she slips on her robe; she opens the door.

Standing there in the hall as if he's about to enter her bedroom is old Mr. Morris. At first she is not even certain it's him, this is so unlikely, so outrageous; there is simply someone there. But the eyes tell her, those brilliant blue orbs. Nothing in them threatens. They gaze at her as if he too is stunned, surprised by what he has found, as if he expected to walk in and go to bed as he did on all those nights through all those years of living here with his wife. Five, ten, fifteen seconds they stare at each other and nothing in his face changes. Then there is a change so swift and profound it's as if those fifteen seconds never existed.

He smiles, as a young man smiles at a young woman, to appeal, to entice, to tease — a lover's look. Never do his eyes leave hers and his face is radiant with pleasure and happiness and loving tenderness. He is overjoyed now to see her.

He says, his voice a little hoarse and croaking, "So then, have you found that earring? I've come to look for it."

She understands. It takes a moment, but she understands. And she returns the smile. It would be impossible not to return it, he is so hopeful, so expectant so elated.

"You step back," he says. "You watch and see. I'll find it."

Why blast his dream? He is harmless. She will play along for a while and then call the daughter to come pick him up, or walk him home herself. Angelica moves aside and allows him to enter. He takes her hand; she turns with him and they step to the foot of the bed. He glances around and lets out a long light sigh.

"You know," he says. "This room could use some paint, some curtains, a new rug. You'd like that, wouldn't you?"

"Oh, yes," she says.

They gaze at each other; they share a look of friendship, of contentment, of devotion. He seems suddenly youthful and strong.

"So then, let me get busy," he says.

He urges her to sit on the bed. He hangs his cane on the footboard. He stalks the room, looking high and low in a jesting mock search for the earring.

"You might try there," she says, pointing. "In the corner."

He pulls the chair away and goes down cautiously on all fours. He looks, he probes with his fingers, he shuffles about on his hands and knees. He moves along the wall, searching, probing with his fingers in the shadows. It is all exaggerated. He is playacting for her; he is entertaining her. He looks beneath the dresser, bending low, but soon he lifts his old body and shakes his bald head, glancing back at her with a teasing-serious face.

"No?" she says. "Then try there, beneath the chest."

He shuffles over, but finds nothing of course. He shuffles all around, searches everywhere, until their eyes are glowing with joy and their shoulders are trembling with quiet laughter.

"Oh, my aching knees," he says and puts out a hand.

She helps him up. He sways on his feet, seems dizzy, disoriented. She guides him to the bed and helps him to sit. He looks up at her, moving his head slowly, and, still holding her hand, he draws her to his side. Their thighs are touching through the material of her robe, his baggy trousers.

"Next week," he says. "Next week, I'll buy you another earring. What's an earring?"

She nods approval, and then he is holding her in his arms. He is hugging her, embracing her. It is a moment she has known before, has longed to know again, and she receives him warmly. They pat each other's backs, rest their heads against the other's shoulder. In the dim light they sit like this for a long time, saying nothing, only touching. She can feel his heart beating in his withered old chest, beating in time to hers.

THE
SULFUR-COLORED
STONE

The words that haunted the boy's mind as he walked through the woods that fine spring morning would live with him for the rest of his days.

"Depression," the men kept saying.

"Ruin," his father had mentioned, and, "Poorhouse."

This had come from his mother: "We won't take charity, you see. I'd sooner die."

"Bread lines," he had heard from another and tried hopelessly to imagine such a thing.

"The newspapers say it's thousands, millions."

"And hoboes everywhere, in the trains, on our streets."

"What's a hobo, Mother?" the boy had asked and she looked at him sharply, wondering how to answer. She said, "Hush."

He thought of the words as he passed over the familiar trail, under the tall pines, the blooming redbuds and dogwoods that his mother loved so much, the occasional white oak, the hickories, the sweet gums, walking among the shrubby yaupon that caught at the wool of his short pants and knee socks. He repeated the words to himself, walking on, mindless of the warm roasting pan which he carried before him by its handles. He said the words out loud to the rising sun, golden and brilliant beyond the leaves and branches and trunks of the well-known trees along the creek. And the words, the sound of his own ten-year-old and puny voice, returned to him in echo like something huge and formless and forever terrible.

"Even in Texas," he repeated, uncertain which of the men had said it. Was it Daddy or Uncle Buster or Mr. Ramsey? "They even let it come to Texas, to these woods, dang 'em."

The thought of such an outrage halted him. He looked down at the roasting pan; he looked out into the woods; he remembered everything. "No, it's a lie. We'll be back, I'll bring us back."

Then he ran. Carefully, in short kicking-out steps, like a boxer in training, he skipped over the trail. At the creek's log bridge he slowed, sidestepped, and paused on the other side to look, just to look and listen, to remember the place.

He ran through the hollow where the marsh smelled of old dead things, and here he quickened his pace, for he hated the marsh and its smell. At the top of the hill he stopped.

Smoke puffed lazily from the chimney of the cabin and spread upward through the morning-still trees and the striking rays of the sun, glowing golden just beyond the cabin so brightly now that the cabin itself existed in its meager clearing only because he knew it existed. The boy had seen it there every day, every morning and every evening, through four of his ten short swift years. Something moved in the shadow of the cabin's porch. Though he could not see what it was that moved, he knew.

That's him, the boy thought. Just like always. Waiting. The old slave. Waiting.

He ran again. At the bottom of the hill, moving into the clearing, he stopped abruptly, hesitated and walked ahead with a kind of formal purpose in his steps and his attitude, carrying the blue pan before him with care, holding the pan out as an offering to the old man when he reached the cabin's porch.

"Well, it's about time," came the black voice from the black face, as old as any voice and any face he had ever heard or seen.

"So this is it," said the voice, still powerful, still deep, but not unfriendly. The old man loved the boy, though the boy was not to realize this until years later when he reached an age at which he thought he understood love, thought he understood everything he needed to understand.

"So y'all going today," said the voice, softer now and with tenderness, and with regret too. The boy nodded his head.

The old man took the boy's offering and with one hand balanced it like a platter. He said, "Morning, Walter," as he did every morning, had done every day for each of those four incredibly swift years. It was their way with each other, this ritual, a way born in uncertainty, established in distrust, nurtured in a kind of ancient solicitude that kept the one always up, up on the porch, and the other always below, below the porch; it was their way, a pact almost, a manner born in the distance that difference fosters, grown now into a certain grudging but admiring respect.

"Morning, Mr. Hick," returned the boy and he removed his cap. If the old man had owned a hat he too would have removed it. The black hand reached toward the white head in an old and remembered instinct of youth, but nothing was there.

"I thank you, as always," said the voice on the porch.

"You're welcome, as always," came the other, smaller, thinner, from below.

The one above spit out his quid and a long black line traced from his mouth to the dewy dust beyond a porch plank that the boy saw was dark and spotted from no telling how many thousands of misses. He wiped his chin with the sleeve of his yellow-stained and stinking undershirt and then sat down on the weathered-gray and backless pew taken forty years before from a burned-down Baptist church in Karankawa and brought here to stay.

With a great teasing kind of ceremony, he removed the top of the pan, glanced with a grin at the boy, held up his nose to catch the rising aromas and then took out the two covered bowls and the new plug of tobacco. One bowl contained his breakfast, honey-sweetened oatmeal and biscuits made by the boy's mother's hands, and one contained his lunch, an apple, four biscuits and a piece of ham, also prepared by the hands of Elvira McIntyre.

"She says for you to just keep the dishes," said the boy.

"You tell her thank you, will you?"

"Yessir."

"Won't you have a seat, young Walter?" asked the black voice. This too was part of their way with each other and every morning the boy refused, adding, "But thank you just the same."

He ate then, with fierce delight, for the boy's mother could make even oatmeal and biscuits taste like the delicacies of Houston. And the boy watched intently as each

mouthful found its destination. Why he waited and
watched was never clear to him, though he would think
later that he understood this too. This too was part of
their way with each other. It would be indelicate, wrong,
perhaps even an insult simply to bring the old man's feed.
All his life the boy (and later as a man and even later as
an old man) would hate to eat alone and he would hate
for those he loved to have to eat alone. So he stood there
below the porch and watched, even though time that
Sunday was precious and he would be punished by his
mother's tongue for making his family wait on him. They
had much to do and far to go.

The huge lips of the man stopped moving; the
still-strong muscles eased in the face, the shoulders, even
the legs. He had finished. Belching first, he said, "Care for
coffee?"

"Ain't got time today, Mr. Hick. "Without a word the
old man rose from the pew, disappeared into the cabin and
then, after a short while, returned. There were two cups in
the hands that led the huge stooped body from the darkness of that deep never-seen interior to the lighted porch.
The boy took the offered cup without saying a word, for
his mother did not yet allow him to drink coffee. They
sipped quietly and the coffee warmed them and opened
their thoughts.

"So today's it, huh."

"Yessir."

"Going to Houstontown."

"Yessir."

"The big old city."

He grinned shyly.

"Never to return."

The boy hesitated before saying it. To lie even about
deep, unspoken intentions was to sin.

"Yessir," he said again.

Had his mother, his father, his brother, his sisters, his uncles, his aunts, his neighbors in Karankawa ever heard him say "yessir" to any black man but this one, he would have been beaten (mildly: a slap, a push, a cuff, with taunts) and his mouth washed out with soap. So he said it self-consciously, always aware that he was saying it. But Mr. Hickory was . . . was different.

"Your daddy — well, how's he doing?"

"Out of bed now."

"But still out of work too. . . ."

"Yessir."

"Pity. What a pity. A man at the prime of life and with all you little responsibilities."

The boy was silent over this, listening, watching.

"Takin' you to Houstontown."

"Yessir."

"Thinks there's work there, does he?"

"Yessir, he does."

"And gonna give up all this — one-hundred and sixty acres of East Texas bottom land that's his for the waiting, nothing more."

The man sipped his coffee and shook his head over the absurdity of it, and the boy looked around as if he could see all of the quarter-section of land that the old man owned, had owned for five of the boy's puny lifetimes, had come by in the same way he came by his freedom at the age of twelve. "A gift." That's how the boy's people put it. He had heard the stories all his life, passed back and forth between the adults in disbelief: how a colored man, a colored man, mind you, who couldn't read or write except for the scratching of his name on official documents (R. Hickry) had so faithfully served the local doctor in the years after the war in which the boy's grandfather had fought with "honor" and "distinction" and "cunning" for the South — yes, the South, they called it — the war in which his grandfather's brother who remained behind in Indiana had betrayed, betrayed them all, by fighting — what, where, how? He remembered only, Blue Belly. And then the slaves were free. And Mr. Hickory served the doctor in ways the boy never understood, not until so many years later when he thought he understood everything. And the stories said, in the voices of disbelief: ". . . and the doc gave that old nigra the best piece of land for fifty miles around." Left it to him, they said. Willed it to him. Can you believe? Just imagine. The doc was out of his head by then.

And there was the secret story too. It was the reason he had come to the cabin that morning, had come to the cabin every morning for four of his ten short and swift years.

"You tell no one, and I'll tell no one," the old man had said that day. "They'll know it all soon enough, when I'm gone."

It was a secret and even to think of it made the boy afraid, afraid that he, like his grandfather's brother ("Your Great Uncle Henry") would betray. And so always the thought of it came to him in the voice of the old man on the porch above him.

"I am old," he had said, speaking to the boy's father and mother, standing below that other porch, the porch of the boy's family's rented house on the outskirts of Karankawa, the house fewer than two miles away from the woodsy Negro smell of the cabin whose porch he now stood below. "An old man," the black voice had said to the boy's parents and he paused then as if considering the enormity of the idea. "I haven't long to live, I'm sure." Though he could not read or write he spoke that day as if he could, in the voice of a preacher or a town Negro who'd gone away and come back educated. "And I have this to offer you." Again he paused and the boy, only six then, clutching his mother's skirts, knew even then that the man was reconsidering it one last time before making the commitment that both races would consider an outrage. "I have no one to care for me. . . ."

The boy's father spoke up then, as he seldom did, quiet, slow, thick-tongued: "That's none of our concern, Rufus."

The old black face smiled. "Not yet it ain't. But listen." The face went serious. "You care for me, feed me, see that I live my days to their fullest potential...." Again he paused before the commitment, and the boy's parents looked at each other, wondering, the boy was sure now, over the word (*potential?*). ". . . You do that for me, and when I'm gone, the land is yours."

Only the four of them knew. The boy knew only by the circumstance of his age; he was the youngest and just happened to be there on the porch that day, clutching his mother's skirts.

Now Rufus Hickory, sitting on the pew on the porch of his cabin in the meager clearing in his beautiful woods, said this: "I have the paper your daddy wrote out. The will, it is called," and the boy remembered that day too, the day after the bargain was made when Mr. Hickory had returned with two others and in the kitchen of the boy's parents' house had signed the paper (R. Hickry) and had said, "Now, you two witness it; put your marks there" (he pointed for the one) "and there" (he pointed for the other) "but don't read a word." The three of them glanced at each other and Mr. Hickory said, "Cain't read no-how." The two signed the paper and Mr. Hickory gave each one a dollar.

"You tell your daddy for me," said Rufus Hickory to

Walter McIntyre Jr. "You tell him that tomorrow morning I gonna walk that trail you walk every day to bring me my breakfast . . . I gonna walk it to see. You tell him this: If there ain't no smoke rising from your chimney, I'll burn the paper. I'll have to." He paused, almost sipped his coffee. "He'll understand."

II

The long period of silence had ended. The pronouncement had been made and thought given to it by the two humans — the large old black one and the small young white one — there in the meager clearing. The sun was up completely now and the coffee dregs in their cups lay still and cold. The boy had to go; he fidgeted and fought the impulse to turn, to run.

"You'll tell him?" asked Rufus Hickory.

"Yessir," said the boy, knowing this was not quite true, for it was his mother waiting on him with her cold stony eyes.

"Make it clear for him that I don't want to but I got to," the man said. "Your daddy always been good to me."

"Yessir, I will."

The old man nodded his white head gruffly in conclusion and they went silent. Rufus Hickory tried to think of the best way to say goodbye to this white boy he had come to know and love over the past four years, the swift years, swifter for him than for the boy. Every morning, every evening: the talk, brief but enough, the imparting of elusive wisdom from age to youth, the imparting of forgotten innocence from youth to age. The boy had been the man's contact with that other age, that other world, one of which he had lost in the natural progression of time, the second of which he had given up for the solitude of these woods, this cabin, after the years of work that had led him nowhere, and the death of his wife. But a man cannot forget entirely and the boy with his news of births and deaths and marriages helped make it real for him again, gave him a life outside the cabin.

The boy searched for an argument, the words to ask: would you not burn the paper? The land, these woods, all he had ever known: his mind refused to see that it was gone from him now.

"There ain't no choice for us, Mr. Hick. Couldn't you wait? Give us time? A few months? I'll bring us back. Please?"

Had his father heard him ask such questions of anyone, much less a black man, he would have been whipped; it had been his mother who had pressured him in secret to try.

"Cain't wait," came the black voice. "How I to do for myself? An old man, broke down like some worthless machine. What I s'pose to do? Chase the possum? The coon?" He looked at the boy for an answer and shifted uneasily on the pew. "Life turns, runs off from you sometimes. Cain't catch it, no-how, cain't pin it down. Now me, this thing — a depression, you call it, they tell you to call it — this thing that was so far off is up close now and just like with y'all that didn't look for it — well, me too and now here it is. Y'all leaving leaves me in the depression, you see. . . ." His mind drifted, and then almost in anger he said, "Now you got to git or your mama be in for you in a big way."

The old man's face, like some huge fruit or vegetable at the county fair, showed the boy nothing human. He knew why. He had seen it before in the faces of adults who had decided something, understood that something inevitable had arrived, and even in love or fondness they became cruel. "Go on!" the old man said.

The boy turned, took a step and then stopped in the dewy dust below the porch. He stood in a triangle of dusty sunlight. He felt the old man's stare. From behind him he heard, "Walter."

It was barely a whisper, barely a breath. But the boy turned again and leapt up onto the porch for the first time in his life. He hugged the old black neck and felt the old black hands on his back and smelled the old black odors of a body born in slavery that had slaved still in freedom and slaved even then to remain alive. It was the first time they had ever touched each other in love and it would be the last time and for the rest of his life the boy (and then the man and then the old man) would recall the moment every time he touched or smelled or even saw rough leather. The smell, the touch, even the sight of a saddle on a horse's back would always remind him that once, long ago, hugging the neck of his family's former handyman, he had wept.

He turned; he leapt from the porch. He ran out of the meager clearing and into the familiar trees of the ancient forest and up the hill and then down the hill, through the marsh and its bitter smell, until he came to the creek. On its bridge he stopped.

Goodbye, deer, he thought, and in his mind there appeared the deer he had once fed from his hand. Goodbye, coons, and possums, and copperheads. Goodbye, hawks. Goodbye, foxes. Goodbye, bears, he thought, for there were still bear in the East Texas woods at that time. "Goodbye, woods," he said.

The call of a mockingbird reminded the boy that he was late. He crossed the log bridge to the other side but stopped again, looked again, reached down and picked up a handful of the black forest dirt. He let the dirt warm in the palm of his hand and considered putting it into his pocket to carry as a reminder of this place, but it would only scatter and soil — and it was then that he felt the stone pressing against the sole of his shoe. He turned the stone with the sole of his shoe, dug at it, picked it out of the dank black earth with his toe and bent down again. It was beautiful, the size of a robin's egg, the color of sulfur. It warmed in his hand. It fit into his pocket easily.

III

All that morning, ever since she had pulled herself from the bed at 4:30 to finish the packing and prepare for the day, Elvira McIntyre had been plagued by the feeling that something was living in her belly, gnawing on her insides. It wouldn't quit and every few minutes she caught herself rubbing, touching, holding with her palm the slight bulge around her navel.

I'm just anxious, she said to herself half a dozen times even before the sun had risen to show that every-thing — the yard, the listing and paintless picket fence, the pitted street out front and the alley behind, her neigh-bors' houses across the street and beyond the alley, the woods that stretched away to the east — Karankawa was still there. She had dreamed herself into a city that night. Was it Houston? She'd never been to Houston; she'd never been to any city larger than Marshall or little Huntsville with its several thousand citizens. That's where old Sam Houston was buried, some of whose blood ran in her veins. This she had been told by her mother, the proud woman from Marshall, the daughter of a judge, the wife of a lawyer who had made a deep mark with his Marshall Land & Surveying Co. They had lived in a huge yellow house with servants.

Didn't they have a duty, an obligation to succeed, for what would the people say who knew that some of the privileged blood of old Sam Houston ran in the veins of her children? No, it was more; they had a right to succeed and no setback such as the one they were now suffering would set them back permanently.

Still, it was an embarrassment and she had not stepped foot outside the house in nearly six months except on Sundays and Wednesday evenings. For what would they think, her neighbors, were she to stoop so low, to be over-whelmed to the point that she allowed herself, her hus-band, her children, to go without God?

"Well, I know good and well what they would think," she said out loud to the window that offered the view of the woods. She had been standing there, looking out, for some time. Then she remembered and said, "Where is that boy?"

The others had gone on in the loaded-down Ford pulling the loaded-down trailer. They had gone on to church — Sunday school would have begun by now — and she had stayed behind to wait for her youngest who had gone to feed that old slave.

If only he would die, now, this very morning, so that the secret pact could be fulfilled. It must be fulfilled, for she knew better than most the value of land. Land was esteem. Land was privilege. And how they had paid: she rising early each morning to prepare the old man's meals and then sending off her youngest, her brightest, the most loyal and wise of the four, to carry it to him through the cold threatening woods and then having to lie to the oth-ers as to his whereabouts each morning and evening. Just imagine what they would say.

And there was another reason why she had sent them all ahead that Sunday morning. Time, a few minutes: to say farewell. Three of her four children had been born in this house. During the good years when the railroad had prospered and Mr. McIntyre had prospered along with it there had been the prospect of a grand future. No great wealth, certainly, but at least enough for comfort and respectability. So that children seemed proper. To have children said to the world that they knew what lay ahead and were ready for it. Four children in eight years, raised in this house. She heard the voices, the laughter, remembered the plans she and Mr. McIntyre discussed in their bed at night. Each year they said: save, save hard this year, and next year we'll buy that house on Travis Street which Brother Hames is holding for us, renting now, but holding till we can get up the down payment, bless his heart. And they planned as well for their children.

John, the eldest, would be a carpenter, a cabinetmaker, perhaps even a jewelry maker; and Julia, beautiful and fierce and wild, she would marry well if they were careful; Irene, poor Irene, almost blind from reading, she would be a fine teacher.

And then there was Walter, Walter, Jr., who could compute a row of figures faster than an adding machine, whose fourth grade term essay was found so worthy as to be published in the local newspaper, who even then had saved enough nickels and dimes from odd jobs and bottle refunds that his account at First Karankawa rivaled the accounts of some families. There was no telling with Walter; he could do anything. She longed to see him just then.

"Where *is* that boy?" she said to the window.

IV

As if in answer to her question he appeared. He emerged from the woods, running. He ran through the open gate, across the yard and around the house. It was time finally and she set her face to an attitude of cold stone. She would meet him with this face, absolutely cold and objective, a judge's face, almost cruel, not because she wanted to; she had to. It was the only way to keep him, to keep him hers as long as possible. The will achieves and her will would see to it that they — the McIntyres — prevailed.

And here he was, standing boylike in the tall narrow doorway of the empty room where just the day before there had been nine pieces of her mother's fine furniture, handed down to be cared for, tossed yesterday like so much cordwood onto that trailer Mr. McIntyre had purchased with half of what they had left. The boy stood there, holding his cap, silent, waiting for her to speak.

"To tarry is a sin," she said with her cold stony voice, the voice to match the face, the attitude. "Did you know that?"

"Yessum," he said, lowering his eyes, turning his cap.

Her heart heaved in her chest, for she longed to go to him and stoop before him and hug him to her as most women would have done upon a son's return. He looked like something made of china and painted by hands that knew exactly what it is about a boy that makes a mother's heart heave.

"Then why were you so long in returning? Why did you make us wait? You see that the others have had to go on without us."

"Yessum."

"Tell me. Tell me why."

He thought of the stone in his pocket and thought that was the answer, the stone and the woods and the deer and everything else in the woods, but he knew it was not the answer she wanted. He thought he should say this place, that place out there, those woods which I'm not sure I can bear to leave — they kept me. This is what he should have said, but it would not do.

"Tell me," she said.

"I'm a sinner and I ask God's forgiveness."

It was the abject voice of abject humility he had learned so well. It was easier to be abject in the face of unreason.

"Did *he* keep you?"

"Yessum," he lied, very quietly.

"How? Tell me."

"You told me to ask — "

"Hush, now."

He squirmed, boylike, against her unreason.

She said, "Well?"

He knew. The boy knew what she wanted, wanting it without the degrading need to ask. "He said, 'no.' "

Her face of cold stone became colder and stonier. It was what she had expected, but again her heart heaved in her chest and for a moment she forgot herself. "He won't give us any time?"

The boy, eyes down, shook his head under his mother's gaze.

"Go and wash your face," she said and turned to the window for the last time. As the sounds of water pulsed through the pipes above her she looked out upon the yard, her fig tree, like an enormous teardrop, the listing and paintless picket fence, the woods that would have made them privileged.

She said, "Lord, be with us," as the pipes went silent.

They met at the front door, he looking up, expectant, still timid, she looking down with a faraway abstraction in her eyes. She nodded once toward the door and with one hand atop the other he slowly opened it. She stepped out gracefully, ladylike, with pride. They looked at each other again. This time she smiled.

"You look quite handsome today," she said.

The boy's hand felt like something retrieved from long ago. Small, cool, moist, it caused her own hand to close around it tightly and to lead it gently. The hand was so sweet that she wanted to taste it, to touch it to her lips and she remembered when the small hand was even smaller, even sweeter.

They walked the twelve blocks to the church without speaking and without seeing anyone they knew. Everyone they knew was in church already and the street was quiet but for the songs of the birds and the diminishing rumble of the morning train which came to them from the tracks across town. The pure sunshine in the elms and oaks, the pure empty taste of the March air, the pure and perfect stillness — it all spoke of one thing: her Sunday.

There was the car and behind it the humiliating trailer, covered with a tarpaulin the color of an engineer's overalls. They had parked it, thank goodness, at the farthest corner of the church's gravel lot, under Sister Lamb's pecan tree.

Mother and son went up the steps. The voices from within the white building were doing great violence to her favorite hymn.

"Goin' afar," they sang as if the words were so much wheat being processed, "upon the mountain, bringin' the wanderer back again . . ." and they went on wavering through the verse.

She and the boy waited at the double doors in the tiny foyer for the congregation to finish the hymn which she knew by heart and in her mind she sang along with them. Then it ended and she heard the shuffling feet, the rustling of Sunday clothes, the coughs of the men as they sat upon the hard polished pews and prepared themselves for the sermon that would go on too long. She reached for the door, but an ugly image of Brother Jordan, the preacher, rose in her mind and she stopped herself. As the boy gazed up at her, wondering, she imagined the preacher's broad condemning face looking out at her from above the pulpit. It would condemn her as a failure were she to walk in now, late, especially now, now that they were leaving. To fail, the face would say, is to sin and you have failed us all.

She turned with the boy's hand still in hers and led him away. The serene morning beckoned to her, drew her from the shadowy steps onto the bright and silent sidewalk. Up the street they walked to the corner where they could glimpse Karankawa's tiny downtown square. She led them away from the square to the street behind the church and they turned again. She walked as if in a trance. The boy saw this, felt it in the way she led him onward and, though his hand had begun to ache in her grip, he said nothing, did nothing but follow.

They turned again, into a wide alley behind the familiar houses of the neighborhood. That's when they saw the man.

He was digging in a garbage can, his head almost hidden inside the opening. The boy and his mother stopped and quite suddenly, as if sensing their presence, the man looked up, straightened himself beside the garbage can. His clothes were old and torn and dirty and the toe of a sock jutted through a hole in one of his gray shoes. His whiskered face, like his clothes, was old and torn and dirty, and there was something more. It was in the eyes and the boy understood it as fear, a hungry kind of fear, a wizened terror, the likes of which he had never seen before and he pulled on his mother's hand trying to back away. The man backed away too, like a spooked animal, glancing around, crouching, and then he ran, casting looks at them over his shoulder. He stumbled, then ran again.

His mother said, "Get, get!" as she would to a dog. The

boy felt her shiver and her free hand rose by instinct to protect her neck. "A white man," she muttered in her confusion.

Quickly, turning, almost stumbling herself, she led them out of the alley then in the direction they had entered and they retraced their steps toward the church. These new steps were much faster, more erratic; these steps jarred the body and hurt him.

"Mother?" the boy asked after a proper interval, with great courage. "Was that man a hobo?"

"Hush," she said and hurried onward.

V

Rufus Hickory lowered his heavy body from the porch of the cabin and walked through the meager clearing into his woods. The boy had been gone for some time now. The old man had given great thought to what his leaving meant but had found no answer.

There was a place he always went at such moments to talk to God. He did not believe in the God of the Christians anymore; he believed in a kindhearted God who listened without condemnation, who longed to help the troubled whether he could or not.

Along the narrow path through the trees he went until he came to the bridge over the creek. This was his special place.

He sat down and he prayed, asking for guidance and deliverance. It was all still a mystery to him, vague and troubling, but he felt calmer in his heart and thought the answer would be revealed to him in time. Tomorrow perhaps, when he went to see for sure that they had gone, or the day after.

He rose and walked across the bridge to the other side. It was here that the deer came to be fed. He stood there listening, thinking, until he felt something pressing against the sole of his boot and he looked down. Footprints, left by small shoes, marred the rich black soil. Walter had stopped here. Walter had taken something from the soil.

Rufus Hickory moved his foot and saw the stone that must have been loosened by Walter's digging. The stone was the color of sulfur. It warmed in his hand when he picked it up.

VI

The service had ended. The congregation had risen, moved and milled in the foyer and was spilling onto the steps. There was quite a lot of talk about the McIntyres, Elvira especially, and shaded glances given the old Ford and its trailer parked in the far corner. Was she so proud, so haughty as to deny them their goodbyes? Could she not face them now that the day had arrived? Why, for heaven's sake, was she sitting there like a queen in her place in the car with her youngest beside her?

Mr. McIntyre and the three eldest did their part — the kisses, the handshakes, the farewells — and Mr. McIntyre explained an illness in the boy that had kept his wife away. But he was not one to say much, so the questions of the women went mostly unanswered and none was so bold as to venture toward the car.

Only the preacher, Brother Jordan, carrying his Bible, followed when the four McIntyres had finished with the goodbyes and the hugs and the handshakes and left the steps behind.

"Well, Elvira," said Brother Jordan through the car window. "We'll miss you and your good work here."

She smiled coldly, to herself, without looking at him.

"I hope Walter is better."

"Yes, he's fine," she said, again without looking at him. "Just a touch of something," she lied and felt the cold reproaching stares of her children warm upon her face.

Then Mr. McIntyre had cranked the car and as it grumbled all of the family got in and seated themselves, the three eldest in back and the parents like bookends beside the youngest in front. The preacher, his face grave and pious, touched the mother's arm in the window and said, "Find peace in prayer, Elvira."

"I have all the peace I need," she came back sharply.

But then she looked at him. His broad earnest face carried no condemnation. His large blue eyes were sad at her leaving, sad over the turmoil in her heart. They had known each other for twelve years; she had served as his secretary on several occasions and she had taught Sunday school at one time; he had come to the house every day during Mr. McIntyre's recovery and he had baptized each of her three eldest. Why, in a year or so he would have baptized her youngest, too, but of course now it would be done by someone else, a stranger, off there in the city.

"I'm sorry," she said quite suddenly. "I'm sorry for everything," she said with a strained and painful passion, awkward and beseeching, gazing into his bland but questioning face. She reached out for his hand but found that he had already backed away. "Don't, Mama," whispered her youngest, leaning close up behind her; all the others were silent in their confusion and their shame. She felt again their stares full of reproach and an overpowering weakness seemed to drain the blood from her arms; she laid them gently in her lap as the well of emotion in her chest began to overflow. Against her cheek she felt something, a kiss, and in her ear she heard something: "Don't, Mama."

Her eyes tried to look at him in tenderness, her heart tried to let her smile, but her God would not allow it.

"Let's go, Walter," she said. And then the car was moving, the world was moving, though every heart and tongue was still, and the children waved to the few waving members of the congregation still gathered on the church steps. "Goodbye," they called.

Through the town they went one last time. There was more activity now. A few cars around the square, people strolling on the sidewalks, a father and son tossing a ball in the weedy lot of the yellow-brick schoolhouse. It was all so familiar and yet already so distant, so remote from them, as if they were travelers from far away and just passing through this little town on their way to something else. No one spoke; they had nothing to say except to themselves. Only one of them would ever see Karankawa again and when he returned, as an old man scarred and bitter and full of regret, it would appear to him exactly as it had that day, upon his leaving, as if the place would never change, could not change, as if he himself were still the same.

Young Walter, sitting on a small wooden lunch basket between his parents, said out loud, with childish fire and conviction, and to the astonishment of the others, "I'll bring us back, you'll see. It's our land, his'n mine. I'll bring us back."

His mother stroked his hair to calm him, to correct him, but he held tightly the sulfur-colored stone in his palm.

BRINGING
JOBOY BACK

For more than an hour there had been only the wildflowers. She hadn't noticed them at first, before the morning overcast had burned away, before the spring sunlight had drawn out their colors and shapes. But now she concentrated on them as something distinct and wonderful in the otherwise down-dragging landscape along the highway. The flowers stood in small clumps on both low-sloping walls of the ditch and in thinner patches, less often, under the regiments of trees in the forest beyond. Every so often she would see a cluster of three or four reaching up innocently from a crack in the pavement and each time she had the urge to pick these before the tires of a truck or a car could crush them.

I ain't got the time, she would think, *ain't got time*, and she went on quickly as if turning from a condemned animal.

The dome of the courthouse in Karankawa appeared beyond the next hill. *Good,* she thought. *I'm getting close now.* The dull nub, shining in the morning mist, rose above the trees in jerky stages as if it were moving instead of Ruby. From somewhere in the near woods came the high whining gnarl of a chain saw and she realized that she'd been listening to it for several minutes without hearing it. The sound, pervasive and encompassing, grew louder, closer, with each step she took in the roadside dust.

She stopped — listening, panting. Cocking her knee, pulling up her foot, she touched the shoe, a flat dusty white under her black hand. Her fingers left three distinct stripes. *I will wait,* she thought, *until I get there,* and the hair at the nape of her neck bristled as she sensed something coming up the road behind her. This time it was a bus. She glanced up just as its smoke-fouled wash rushed over her body and blew up her skirt. The bus crested the hill and descended, vanishing in a smoky glide toward Karankawa, and she wondered if it was the one that went on to Huntsville. She smoothed down her skirt and, clutching the white purse under her arm, she set out again, watching the dome rise and hearing the chain saw whine in the woods.

Cutting had been Joboy's job on the county crew, years ago when she was a girl, seventeen, eighteen, still tending house for her father. Joboy was her third man, much older than the others, and she had sometimes gone with him when he worked, waiting for him in the truck, listening to the men curse and joke and hearing the gnarling, the rising and falling scream of the saws from up in the boughs of the trees. Afterwards they would go to the Tiptop Inn and they would tap their feet to music, dance on the spongy-rotten floorboards, drink beers, laugh with each other.

Then her father died, laid in a grave beside her mother on a wooded hill, and Joboy stayed away for months. She lived for a while with her Aunt Octavine, who had never married, who had worked as a secretary at the Baptist church in Harristown for twenty-eight years and sang hymns in the bathtub every night, her voice high and squeaky like a squirrel's staccato bark. "Sing with me, Ruby," she would squeak. Finally Joboy came one day, scraping his feet against the porch slats and turning his hat in his hand.

"I got a place to stay and two-hundred dollars," he said. "And a pickup truck. And I got a bag of groceries."

Her aunt grunted from behind the screen door. "Get away, you." Then to Ruby: "He's a shifter, that's all. Better wait."

But Ruby said, "Let me get my things."

He said, "There's something you ought to know." His voice was serious, straightforward, and she paused. Octavine whispered, "Don't, Ruby," through the screen.

Joboy said, almost proclaimed, "I've got a daughter, a little one, going on eight." It rang like a confession.

Ruby stood still, watching him over her shoulder. She said, "So did my daddy." She glanced at her aunt, their faces only inches apart, separated by the mesh of wire. "I'll get my things." She slipped past Octavine to pack her bags and slipped past her again to leave. "Don't, Ruby," had come the whisper.

She walked on, her feet aching in the seldom-worn shoes. The road dipped sharply into a ravine and the dome of the courthouse in Karankawa fell away beyond the tree tops.

They had married, she and Joboy — no church ceremony, no license, no ring, only vows exchanged in front of a preacher friend. They had all been together. That's when she had lived with Joboy and little Marcene, whom she did not like but had tried to love because she was Joboy's flesh and blood whose mother, he had said, was off in Houston. For two years they had stayed in a house in the woods not three miles from the house in which Ruby was born, and Joboy worked off and on, gone almost all the time chasing jobs, and she cooked and cleaned and swept and took care of Marcene, barely ten years younger than Ruby herself. It was mostly good, but not always.

"You ain't my Mama, you ain't," Marcene would say.

"Go on now, child, and do as I tell you."

"I won't."

They would separate, each pouting, until Joboy returned and Marcene would get to him first as he came into the yard and she would sound her arguments against Ruby and he would come in and glower. Other times, she didn't know why, she would take to herself in the bed for hours until he came to her.

"What you be wanting, woman?" he would say. "She's a child, why you act this way?"

"She ain't my child."

"She's our child."

"No, you know better."

He'd say, "You better get used to it, gal," and he always left in the morning. He started staying away for days at a time, and at home there was only Marcene. Then Joboy came in that night sweating the powerful odor of fright and confusion. He packed a paper sack with some clothes. He said at the door, "I'll be gone awhile." She heard "armed robbery" a few days later and the next time and the last time she saw him was at the courthouse.

The gray-green dome was in full view now and houses lined the road, the outskirts of town. A dog bounded snarling up to a fence. A voice from within the house behind called, "Hey, there!" and the dog stopped, slobbering, eyeing her as she walked.

Joboy had worn blue faded overalls with numbers on the breast pocket the day of the trial. She remembered the judge saying, "I hereby sentence you to five years incarceration at the State Penitentiary in Huntsville," and the bash of the wooden hammer and then a deep, chilling silence. Joboy had looked back at her with his pretty, dark eyes, so frightened and far away.

She was in town. The chain saw had gone quiet, but she glimpsed the glass doors of the courthouse, like big silver eyeglasses watching her. There were stores and restaurants around the square, and she lingered. Televisions flashed at the Western Auto. Big-cushioned couches beckoned at Sal's Furniture Store. Frilly summer dresses graced handsome mannequins at Lilly's Boutique, where a young white woman was pinning up the hem of a yellow frock in the display window. Ruby paused, looking in. She often imagined herself living in the city with a closetful of Holiday Fashions like the ones she had seen in the catalogues, and maybe a car and maybe one of those little apartments she'd heard about that had carpets and a garbage disposal. And Joboy'd have a job doing construction — he could do all sorts of things — and they'd have their own bedroom furniture. She wanted to go inside the store, but the woman in the window glanced up at her with a face that told her not to. *Ain't got time, anyway.*

She walked around the courthouse. The granite building loomed above her with its round-topped windows and high eaves, and she remembered the day she had gone inside. Joboy, his elbow in the grip of a deputy, had come to the rail in the courtroom before they led him away. She could smell him, oily and sweaty, and his overalls didn't fit him at all. He kissed her on the cheek, his lips rough and quivering, and he leaned into her ear: "She be yours now, take care. She's yours." That was three years ago next month and she had memorized the letter.

20 February 1972
Dear Ruby

I am getting out early on good behavior. May 16. Come here to the gate wait for me do not come inside and then we will stay the night in town before going back. Don't bring Marcene.
Joboy

The letter, already yellowing and ripped from two months of handling, lay neatly folded in the purse under her arm. It was only the second letter she had received in the time he had been away while she and Marcene lived in the little room off the kitchen at the Livermores', and she had not seen him, never going to visit. His first letter had said not to. *This is no site for you and most important not for Marcene. Stay away.*

So she worked for the Livermores — almost thirty months now — wearing the tight-fitting maid's uniform that Mrs. Livermore had bought her and putting away the "good money" she got each month in the white purse. She kept her wages in a separate compartment of the purse from the "little extra" that Mr. Livermore slipped into her pocket on his "special occasions."

She carried $800, enough to get away. She would have to convince Joboy, make him see that they should get away, to the city, any city. But the Livermores had promised to give Joboy a job on the ranch when he got out. Joboy liked ranch work and, except for the lying and the worry and the sweat of that old man as he pawed her, it wasn't a bad life with the Livermores. They had given her work and a place to stay with Marcene when she had

had no place else to go; and they had given her the day
and the night off to go to Huntsville and bring Joboy back.

Ruby went up the block to the bus station. The man at
the ticket window said she had missed the first bus; it
would be forty minutes. She paid and took a seat beside a
woman with a suitcase and a small boy who ogled her with
cheerful blue eyes. She smiled at the boy and then took
out her handkerchief, a lavender color with maroon pip-
ing. Propping her right foot on the edge of the bench, she
wiped off the dust that had turned the shoe gray. Then she
bent low and wiped the left one.

II

"Hurry, Marcene," Ruby had said that morning. Her
voice butted against the bathroom door. "I'm late and you
got to stay with Mrs. Livermore today." The girl said nothing. She'd been quiet for two solid days. Ruby knocked on
the door. "Hurry, girl. Mr. Livermore's waiting on me."

The door opened. Marcene stood there, looking, pouting. Ruby glanced over Marcene's head and saw herself in
the mirror: the glaze of still-sleepy eyes, the rough morning face and the odd slant of the brow, the hair cleaving to
one side of her head.

"Are you through, girl?"

Marcene squeezed by Ruby and threw herself onto the
bed. "Why I got to stay with that old lady for?"

"You know why. I'm getting your daddy today."

"Why I can't go?"

"You know that too. Now quit your surliness and get
dressed."

Marcene's lips pouted. Ruby stepped into the bathroom
and closed the door. There had been a boy lately. Ruby
had seen them together, getting off the school bus, laughing, touching, talking in the long minutes in the light dust

that swirled up and remained after the bus chugged away. And she had come home bruised one day, a swell under her eye, saying that she had had a fight with a girl. But there was the boy, tall, lanky and pretty, like Joboy, and Ruby had told her to wait.

"There's lots and lots of time."

Then Marcene: "Wait for what?" Going real surly: "What-chu mean?"

Then Ruby: "Just wait, please, you'll know soon enough," but thinking, *Should I tell her now, is now the time?*

Ruby thought, *I can't today, and what would I tell her?* She washed her face, combed her hair, sprayed cologne on the long line of her neck. The slip was pearly white against her skin.

Three knocks banged through the outer door — the bedroom door — muffled, snappy, the hand of Mrs. Livermore. "Come on, now, Ruby." The old woman's voice pierced the door like the clash of pots and pans in a sink. "Mr. Livermore can't wait all morning."

The door opened. Marcene yanked the bed covers up to her neck and let out a sharp squeal. Mrs. Livermore, her dark dyed hair sticking to her forehead in curls, walked through the room as if inspecting it for something. "Good morning, Dear," she said to Marcene. "Aren't you cute. You little ones are always so cute in the morning." Marcene gave Ruby a puckish, closed-lip smile.

"I'll be right there," Ruby said.

"Hurry," said Mrs. Livermore, marching out to the kitchen.

"Close the door," Ruby whispered. She went back to the bathroom, brushed her teeth, but could see in the mirror that the door was still open. "I said close that door." She strode out of the bathroom, flung the door shut. "Listen to me, girl."

Marcene's little tongue shot out of her mouth and disappeared again. "I don't got to listen to nothing you say."

Ruby stood still, shaking her head at Marcene. "I ain't got time for this. I just ain't got time." She took her Sunday dress from the bedstead and slipped it over her head, shimmied into it. "Now you mind Mrs. Livermore today or you really be in for it. Hear me?" Marcene's lips pouted. "Hear me?" The girl nodded.

Ruby stepped into her shoes and collected her purse from the closet. She took out a five-dollar bill for Marcene. The girl looked at the bill as if it were dirty. "That's not to spend, you hear. It's just in case. In case something happens and you need a little. Keep it and give it back to me tomorrow." Marcene threw the bill to the floor. Ruby picked it up. "Take it." She shook the bill. "Take it, I said." Marcene took it. "Now get dressed, and be sure to press your nice one for your daddy tomorrow."

Marcene got up and went to the closet, took down her dress, threw it on the bed. Ruby watched the girl's naked body, legs slender, little nubs where breasts would soon form, and she briefly glimpsed her future as a woman. *There is pain and blood, gal,* she thought, *and it's the same for all of us.*

"Look, child," she said. "It be only one more day and he'll be home. Things will be better, I promise."

Marcene, calmer, standing still above the dress on the bed, glared straight back at her. Staring at each other, they each waited. And then, like a cat springing for a lizard, the girl moved, letting out a tiny sound, and in two strides was before Ruby, her arms around the soft waist, her face pressed against the jutting bone of Ruby's shoulder. She clung, her breaths coming in raspy whimpers, nearly cries. "Ruby," she said. "Ruby."

The woman hugged the girl's neck and lay her cheek against the pillow of hair. She smelled the sweet-sour morning odor of the slender body and felt the pressure of ten little fingers in her back. She heard, "Ruby," cry-like and distant. She held her. They swayed gently, and Ruby thought, *Yes, this is the way it is. There is pain and blood and the future and the worry and it is always the same.* But she said, "Now now, child." Cooing now. "He'll be home tomorrow and things'll be better, I promise."

In the kitchen the old woman sang, "Hurry, hurry!" Ruby hurried out. The car — the big Lincoln — was idling in the driveway and she could see Mr. Livermore, shadowy and distant behind the windshield, both hands on the wheel. She opened the back door.

"No no," he said. "Up here." His hand patted the seat.

She got in, smoothed out her dress. He looked at her, hard, close, right in the eyes. She glanced at him, just a turn of the head. His eyes were smiling, gentle, but his mouth was even and flat. Something touched her arm and she started to pull away, but then realized what it was. He touched her again, turned his hand over on the seat for her to hold, but she left it alone.

"I guess things are going to change a little now."

"We better be going, Mr. Livermore. I got to catch a bus."

"It doesn't have to change."

She looked at him. Now his mouth was smiling too, almost tenderly, lovingly. He said, "I'll keep him busy."

"Mr. Livermore —"

"I know," he said through his moustache, gray, yellow-stained from cigarettes. They lurched backward and he leaned over the seat, peering back, gripping the wheel with one hand. The car swayed into the road and he whipped it around, started off. He was smiling again, and she knew it was to convince her. He was an old man and she knew that he thought he would have to convince her. "You can have a good life here, Ruby. Just listen to me."

"Right now I got to get to the bus and you're already late."

"Are you listening?"

"I hear you." She paused. "You know he'd kill us both."

"He'll never know." He spoke through his moustache, gripped the wheel with both hands, the car surging forward over the dust.

"I can't do it no more, Mr. Livermore."

"Don't call me that," he said. He touched her thigh and she jerked it away. She could feel his disappointment, the minute shifting of his shoulders, the added pressure on the seat from the deeper slump of his body. "There are ways," he said.

"No. Not no more. I can't no more, I just can't."

She sensed him slump again. There was a frightening finality to it as if he might strike her because he couldn't convince her, in the same way that all men do, even the gentlest of men, who strike out at what they cannot control. She held on to the armrest of her door; he made no movement except for the minute adjustments of the wheel. They were silent as the car rushed on.

At the junction he stopped. The dirt road arched up onto the blacktop, the highway. Something in the silence, the queer stillness, the taut grip of his hands, made her think that he was waiting for her to do something. "I'm late in Bryan," he said.

She snapped her head toward him. His face was serious, grim amid the spots on his fleshy cheeks, those white bushes above his eyes and the lines above them. "But you said you'd take me."

"Sorry," he said with a half-glance, like a child's.

She got out. The car lurched up onto the highway. She walked up, up the arch, and watched it. Crossing the highway, she watched it. The car, wavy as it went away, melted into a shimmer beyond a hill. She started walking. *Hurry. Hurry.*

III

The highway sign said HUNTSVILLE 5. It was cool in the bus — the window was streaked with condensation — but the air was smoky and musty smelling. Then the narrow road between the trees swept open and became a four-lane, the blacktop lined with yellow stripes. Ruby could see the Interstate up ahead, rising in a camelback. Cars and trucks lumbered by on the overpass. There was someone up there on the shoulder: a woman in bright orange pants. And her arm was out. A hitchhiker, going to Houston.

Ruby had been to Houston once when she was a girl. She remembered the tall buildings and the traffic downtown, sidewalks clogged with hundreds of people she didn't know. The people walked swiftly and paid no attention to her, even when she was lost. Her daddy had found her, hugged her, when she had been afraid. He took her into a drug store and gave her a dollar. She bought two little Goody barrettes; she still had one of them.

She glimpsed a sign: HOUSTON 72. *Only 70 miles.* A shadow darkened the window and the roaring of the bus grew louder as it passed under the Interstate. The woman up above disappeared.

They were in Huntsville. She had been through Huntsville a few times. The bus turned several corners and then they were on a thoroughfare with businesses and restaurants, traffic. They went under a canopy. The bus stopped, hissed. The driver stood up and stretched, and then everyone started pushing down the aisle.

Inside the bus station, congested with people, a man told her where the prison was. "Six blocks down, four blocks over."

She started walking. A clock on a bank showed twelve-fifteen. She walked four blocks and turned into a neighborhood of old houses and old trees, tall and thick. Soon the neighborhood on one side of the street gave way to a high, red-brick wall, each brick separate, clean, outlined with mortar. Atop the wall at a corner was a brick block with a pointed roof, like a garage or a shed. Curly wires hung from it and a man in dark glasses stood under the roof. He seemed to watch her as she walked.

She came to a place where the wall veered away from the street like an alcove. There was a high gate and another little house with another man in it. The road that led to the gate curved around a flower bed in the middle of the asphalt. She walked in the shadow of the wall until she could no longer see the little house at the gate or the guard who had watched her.

He'll come soon, she thought, *I'll wait. He'll find me.*

Down the street was a vacant lot, grown up with weeds, and she could see the foundation of a torn-down house. At the front of the foundation were the old porch steps, and a rusty bathtub turned upside down. Scruffy hedgerows shielded the lot from the homes next door. Ruby crossed the street and sat down on the steps. *It won't be long,* she thought, opening her purse and taking out an apple. Mrs. Livermore had said the apples were good this week. She ate the apple and waited.

❧

The sky shone orange and purple like the wildflowers. The sun had just slipped below the trees. Ruby got up and walked toward the gate in the prison wall. She stopped when she saw the man in the little house. He was busy, a telephone in his hand. Now the guard saw her. She could tell by the tilt of his head, his halted motions. She wanted to go up and ask him where Joboy was, but he seemed threatening, menacing in his uniform.

Night lurked just above the trees. In the yard behind the foundation she found a blanket, olive drab, soggy on the corner, pressed flat against the ground and covered with a layer of pine needles. She picked up the blanket and shook it out, carried it to the steps. She wondered if this was the wrong day, if she had mixed up the dates. But she had let Mrs. Livermore read the letter and they had agreed, today was the day. *I'll just wait.*

Then it was night. She looked out at the street once more to see if Joboy were there, but the street dripped with silence under the trees. Letting her head rest on the old doorsill, she laid down and spread the blanket over her body.

Memories, yapping at her mind, kept sleep at bay like the hounds that her father used to run when he hunted. They bellowed and howled until even the thought of sleep crawled out of her and hid in the branches of the trees. She recalled a night, a night only weeks before Joboy had left. "Where you been for three whole days?" she had asked him. He had just come in, it was late.

"Looking for work," he said.

"No, you ain't looking for nothing. I think you found it."

"Let me be, woman."

"Why I should let you be? I'm your wife." He stared at her, his eyes slippery-looking but direct. "Am I not your wife?"

He stared. He walked toward her, staring, and kissed her.

"Answer me, man."

He kissed her, rubbed himself against her. His heavy man odor filled her head and she could just make out his pretty face in the darkened room. He said, "Come on, let's make a baby." She said, "No!" but he touched her, purred for her. And she lay beneath him then. Later, curled warmly in the bed beside him, she had whispered, "Am I your wife, or not?" but he was asleep.

Now, as her own sleep began to numb her body, she realized that the thumb on her left hand had been rubbing the fleshy skin between the knuckles of her bare ring finger. She made it stop and then everything was calm. Once in the night she woke, chilly and frightened, to a sound in one of the shrubs, a rustling, as if someone were shaking it. When she sat up she saw a bird fight its way out of the leaves and strike off into the darkness.

IV

Ruby felt her bones warming. She felt the concrete under her hip and shoulder. She smelled pine needles warming as if in an oven. A car passed on the street, its engine loud, coughing like Joboy in the morning. Her eyes opened to a face, a child's face, peering down at her. The boy held a satchel over his shoulder.

"It's about time," he said. "I've been waiting on you five, ten minutes."

"Where's Joboy?"

His eyes cut into her, questioning. "You better get gone, gal," the boy said. "Daddy says vagrants go to jail."

Her body hurt and her head seemed to be swimming through a deep, dank pool of water. She looked up at the boy. He was twelve, maybe thirteen. Dark curly hair rose from his head like the crown of a chicken. His face was smooth and clean, but colored with curiosity and a vague meanness.

"I'm going," she said and groped for the white purse.

"The police come around and you're in trouble."

"I'm going," she said and stood up, clutching the purse.

Ruby walked into the street, glanced back. The boy was watching her, but soon he started off in the opposite direction. She went to the road through the gate in the wall. There was a new guard in the little house and he saw her, scrutinized her, as if she had arrived to ask him a difficult question.

"Can I do something for you?" he said.

"I'm here to collect Joboy Johnson. He's getting out."

"Johnson. Johnson, you say?" He rubbed the folds of neck under his chin. "Don't know of no Johnson. But hang on."

She could see through the window of the guard shack that he was talking on the telephone. He talked for a long time. "Who are you?" he asked, leaning out the door, the phone in his hand. She told him and he spoke into the phone again. Ruby took out her handkerchief and wiped off her shoes, raising them one at a time to the low curb. She saw him hang up the phone.

"Mrs. Johnson. Somebody's on the way."

Ruby sat on the curb. The guard stayed inside. She marveled at the perfect order of the flower bed in the middle of the asphalt and wondered who tended it. "Mrs. Johnson?" It was another man's voice. He was wearing a dark suit and a tie, but the features of his face blurred in the sunlight behind him.

The man said, "Would you come with me, please."

She followed him through the gate and up a road to a large brick building. Above the door hung the word ADMINISTRATION. He took her through a room crowded with dozens of desks and metal cabinets and then to a smaller room with a single desk and a window full of

sunshine. Another man entered behind them. He introduced himself, Mr. Cutler, and they all sat down.

"So you're Mrs. Johnson," he said. "Ruby Johnson?" He
also wore a dark suit. His bulgy face and neck looked like a
bucket on his thick shoulders. "If we'd of known, we'd of
contacted you."

"Contact me?" She glanced at the other man, sitting
against the wall. He was watching her carefully. She said,
"What about?"

"You see, Mrs. Johnson." He too looked at the other
man, as if for help. But then he said, "Mrs. Johnson,
Joboy's dead."

Something like hot grease slid down her throat into her
stomach and burned. She clutched the purse in her lap
and leaned forward. An image of Joboy's pretty face stood
up in her mind — his eyes were closed, but that was the
only change. She didn't know what to do, so she simply
stared at Mr. Cutler.

He said, "It's been a couple of months now." He talked
for a long time, but she heard only some of what he said.
"There was a fight in the mess hall, you see. . . . There was
nothing we could do . . . he died almost immediately. . . .
If we'd of known, I'm sure we would of contacted you." He
seemed about to say something else, but the words never
formed in his mouth.

"But I'm his wife." It was almost a whisper.

His eyes, little marbles in his bulgy face, stared at her
flatly. "Yes, that's right," he said. "That's what you've told
us." He stared until she turned away. On his desk sat a picture of a huge white horse, its mane and tail standing up
in braids.

"Would you like to see the grave?" Mr. Cutler asked.

The man who had led her into the building now led her
through several offices until they stepped through a door

into the sunshine. "This way," the man said. She followed him down a narrow road, through a gate, and then another, his shoes clapping against the blacktop. The land sloped away on either side to rows of young crops. In the distance she could see figures in white overalls digging at the ground with hoes. Several of them stopped and watched as she and the man walked along.

"This way," he said. They turned into a field and went through another gate in a chain-link fence that came only to her waist. Moving lightly, they stepped between several plain markers embedded in the thick grass, still damp with dew. There were names and dates on each of the markers, and each marker was the gray-green color of tainted copper, like the dome of the courthouse. The man paused in front of one, bending, reading, then another, and then he said, "Here it is."

The marker, shinier, cleaner than the others, said *Joe Henry Johnson, 1932-1972*. Just above the metal plate, standing up in the grass like a marker of its own, rose a tiny clump of wildflowers. The flowers swayed in the simple straight breeze that came and went. She imagined they were growing at about the spot where Joboy's navel was under the ground.

Ruby knelt and gripped the flowers as she would a bouquet. She remembered that Joboy had once brought her flowers, bluebonnets and Indian paintbrushes that grew like weeds along the highways. He had promised, "From now on I'm buying you something pretty every payday." She pulled the flowers out of the grass. She stood. Holding the flowers before her as a bride would, she walked away, feeling the grass tug at her shoes.

"Hold on, there," the man said. "Can I take you somewhere?"

She said, "Yes," and hurried past him up the road toward the building. A light spring had entered her steps

and her breathing came more easily, bringing in more air.
The man followed a few paces behind, working to keep up,
directing her to turn or unlocking a gate. They got into a
car near the big building and he drove them through the
high wall of the prison.

"Where to?"

"Six blocks over," she said, pointing, "and four blocks
up."

When they approached the bus station Ruby told the
man to keep driving. *I can't wait no more*, she thought. *Not
a minute more.* She took out her handkerchief in case she
needed it. *But I'll send her some money and a ticket to meet
me. Yes, that's what I'll do.* They passed the businesses and
the restaurants and the activity of the center of town until
she could see the Interstate up ahead. She said, "Keep
going straight."

Under the freeway she told him to stop.

"Here?"

"I thank you," she said and got out.

Gripping the flowers in one hand, her purse in the
other, she walked out from under the overpass and scrab-
bled up the steep, weedy embankment to the shoulder of
the freeway. *No. I will send her half the money*, she thought.
*No ticket. But half the money. It ought to be hers. And I'll tell
her.* Trucks and cars pounded by on the pavement, pelting
her with a dry hot wind and tiny pebbles. The mid-morning sun pressed on her shoulders. *I'll tell her.* She looked off
down the road that passed under the Interstate in the
direction of Karankawa. *I'll tell her to wait. Wait, I'll say.*
She gazed for a long time at the trees along the highway
and at the vanishing point where the road seemed to drop
into a hole in the earth. Everything, the trees and the
highway and the yellow stripes, verged on a single hazy
image of what she knew was actually there.

She remembered the girl, the small weak cry, "Ruby, Ruby." She thought, *I'll tell her he was no good, a son of a bitch, a waster.* Her throat contracted against something inside it and her eyes burned. She dabbed at them with her handkerchief. *They, none of them, are any good but for pain and blood and for wasting us. I'll explain. And I'll eat, eat everything when I get there, in a nice cafe downtown. I'll be hungry by then. I ain't hungry now, but I'll be hungry then. And I'll explain it to her. I'll write it out in a note and send her the money. Wait, I'll tell her. Wait now so you don't got to wait later, like me.* She blew into the handkerchief. *Wait, I'll say, and then get away.*

Leaning over the guardrail she opened her hand and let the flowers go. They sprinkled down like leaves in autumn. One landed on the hood of a car as it appeared from under the overpass. She watched the car slide in a mirage over the next hill.

Ruby turned, and an image of Houston came to her — buildings, crowds, excitement. She felt strong, as though she had settled something, as though she were about to triumph over everything that had come before in her life, but the feeling made her uneasy. *Go on. Do it.* Carefully, having never tried it before, she put out her hand in the same way she'd seen the woman in the orange pants do it yesterday. She looked beseechingly into every passing windshield, though the reflected sun made them each a blank, hot, silvery mirror, revealing nothing. This was not how she had imagined it. The only faces she could see were in the grills and headlights and bumpers of the furious, speeding cars and trucks, which seemed to jeer at her, paying little attention as they thundered by, and before even a minute had gone she snatched her hand back, curling her fingers into a knot between her breasts. She stood there exhausted, paralyzed, vulnerable and conspicuous, momentarily awed by the deafening sound of the rushing tumult, as shame and humiliation crawled across her scalp, bumped in her chest.

She whispered, "Joboy!" through her teeth. "Why you do this to me?" The blast of a horn told her to get out of the way, and her whole body flinched; her hand reached out for the support of the guardrail. She screamed, "That girl ain't mine," but the howling traffic whisked away the fury of her voice. "She never been mine and will never be. She don't want me. She don't need me." A hubcap freed itself from the wheel of a car, clanged and clattered when it met the pavement, and Ruby turned, looked just in time to sidestep as it spun by within inches of her white shoes. She watched it skip along the shoulder of the freeway like a saw blade gone crazy before throwing itself over the edge of the embankment. And then she was moving, almost running.

Hurry, she thought, sliding and stumbling as she made her way down the steep incline. *Hurry.*

V

The pine trees loomed tall and peaceful in the old forest, on the old sloping and memoried hills, hanging thick and green below the rich expanse of blue spring sky, above the towns and farms and silent cemeteries, their branches twisting out over the shimmering fumes of the county highway along which she walked again, had been walking for half an hour. And from somewhere in the woods she now heard the lonely, familiar sound of cutting, the engine-powered snarl, a constant rhythm, pervasive and encompassing. Like a message in her veins, it told her what she had always known. This place is yours, Ruby Johnson, this and nothing more. Walking on, she came to a highway sign: KARANKAWA 36. *I'll get me something to eat there, and maybe do a little shopping, buy Marcene something pretty.* Turning, scuddling sideways like a crab, she extended her arm, her hand, her thumb — strong-feeling and steady — though another half-hour passed before a logger in his loaded-down truck stopped to pick her up. A big, cheery man with bushy sideburns and bright round eyes, the mingled smells of sweat and sawdust in his clothes, he cajoled her to talk. He questioned her and flirted in a friendly way, and she smiled back at him in a friendly way, or nodded, or shook her head. But she said nothing beyond the necessary in answer to his questions, preferring to sit quietly with her thoughts and her purse and to wait out the trip. They went slowly.

FLOUNDERING

Once, and only once, in the long-ago sober days of my youth, my father took my brother and me floundering. My Uncle Lawrence came along too, and he brought with him a special friend. "My old buddy, Mr. Jack Daniel." He said this often and every time he did my dad would glance at him and they would grin over a secret.

The summer of '64 was my brother's last one at home. He had graduated from high school in the spring, an honor student, and was preparing to start college over in Austin come September, the first in our family on either side ever to do so. He and my father were going through a phase that year: Pure-D anger, fast-boiling and pernicious. A lot of walls were kicked and rarely an evening passed without a furious argument and significant glares.

To repair such damage and try to prevent more of it in the future is why Daddy decided to take us floundering. It was to be a man's outing to do a manly thing, a celebration of sorts, for he was quite proud of my brother. He talked it up for weeks: the three of us together, smelling of salt and sand and masculine sweat, cooking our own food, spearing the big ones.

Floundering, with its special dangerous gear and its dark murky challenge, was something he loved to do, though he had never convinced us of its virtues. He usually went with his best friend, Lyle Dykus, at least once a year.

Mr. Dykus owned an old trailer house on a remote stretch of beach near the little Gulf Coast town of Port O'Connor. They called it The Fish Camp and whenever they spoke of it their voices were glad-sounding and reverential all at once, the way some men speak of some women they have known. Mr. Dykus couldn't get away to go with us that summer, because of trouble in his life. Mrs. Dykus had been arrested on a shoplifting charge, if I recall, and the shock of it, the scandal, the humiliation heaped on his two daughters was keeping him close to home.

"I can't stay," he said the night he dropped off the keys to the trailer. It was late, though the sun was just setting, and he stood below our front porch looking hopeless. He was a short, bald, ready kind of man who always wore khaki pants when he wasn't dressed in a suit for work. "We had a meeting with the lawyer this evening and I better get back. She's pretty upset."

Daddy said, "Holy gosh, Lyle, can't you get away?"

"I surely wish. . ." said Mr. Dykus, but his voice trailed away and the disappointment gleamed in his eyes. In a sideways crawl like a crab he started across the lawn toward his car.

"We'll take good care of the place," my dad called to him. "And bring you back a chestful of flounder."

Daddy waved, just once in an offhand way to let him know not to worry, and then he whispered, "Poor bastard."

That's what he always called Uncle Lawrence too, who was invited to come along only after Mr. Dykus had begged off. Uncle Lawrence was not held in high esteem by the adults in our house. Oh, they loved him — he was my mother's little brother after all and he had what Mother called charm and Daddy called charisma, and he had had a daughter once who died — but it was the sad kind of love you offer a crippled dog.

For one thing he was between marriages at the time, his second, to Aunt Celia, and his third, to Aunt Rose, and for another he was unemployed again. Uncle Lawrence had sold paint, he had sold insurance, he had sold Bibles door to door; he had worked in importing and exporting; and he had once owned a furniture repair shop. He had done just about everything but earn a regular living and this my hard-working, mortgage-paying Methodist parents could never quite forgive.

"Fondness" is the word they used most often, for he was entertaining even if he couldn't always pay his taxes. He preferred to travel and drink tequila and sing songs. He would show up at the house on Sundays, needing a haircut, smiling like a happy stevedore, and after dinner, after a nap, he'd bring in his old battered guitar and play for us, and he told us about the places he had been. They were never the really exotic places you read about; never even very far away — Nuevo Laredo, let's say, or New Orleans — but he charmed us with his charisma.

Derald, my brother, loved him the best. He would sit with Lawrence for hours and listen to him sing Mexican songs in his faltering baritone and watch him strum the guitar, using all five fingers and thumping the box for emphasis. Outside they played pitch or tossed around the football and Derald crawled all over Lawrence trying to tackle him. They laughed a lot together.

Daddy and Derald seldom laughed together then. And I think now that Uncle Lawrence was partly why my father and my brother were going through their phase of anger; he was jealous of Lawrence and his hold on Derald and despised himself for being jealous of such a man, a man he loved and deep down really liked. It twisted him up, made him more severe than his true nature. I remember a number of conversations such as this one:

"Hey, Dad," Derald said once. "Lawrence says a man could do worse than taking off a year and traveling around the country. Maybe a year off before college would do me some good."

"You think so?" Daddy said, putting down the newspaper.

"Well yeah, I do."

"Well, that just goes to show what you know. And Lawrence too. Only bums travel the way Lawrence travels."

"You don't know."

"Yeah, I do. I've seen it, plenty. Now get in there and give those a books a lick and quit listening to your Uncle Lawrence."

"Lawrence isn't a bum."

"He thinks like one."

"You don't know."

"That's the end of it, Der." He picked up the paper again.

"You don't know," screamed Derald, slapping the front page before stomping off to his room. "You don't know anything."

"I know this," Daddy yelled back. "Your Uncle Lawrence is a no-good. . . ." That's as far as he got before mother gave him a sharp look and he caught himself. "The poor bastard."

Later, after I had gone to bed — mine was the upper bunk — Daddy crept in to apologize to Derald, but of course the harm was already done. The next day he announced his plans for our floundering trip to Port O'Connor: "No excuses."

~

Sunrise over Houston was exciting to only one of us and he was driving. The rest of us slept, curled up in various corners of the Chevy. Perhaps the smell of the salt air woke me. I watched the land change, watched it go from dark loam to gritty sand, from narrow blacktop to bright white bridges and causeways. The town itself was nothing but shacks and bait shops and a grocery store, everything weathered and blanched. We stopped for some last-minute provisions and then headed down the beach.

The trailer lay in the dunes like a derelict ship. Streamers of rust ran over its rounded, once-silver shoulders and down its dented sides to the cinder blocks upon which it sat.

Daddy had to kick the door to get it to open and once inside we were greeted with an incredible show. Dozens of mice, squealing and scurrying about, dashed for safe places. They leapt from counters and raced up the airy frayed curtains and spun around in the thin layer of sand on the table top. Daddy looked on, smiling, as if he had arranged this performance just for us.

"As always," he said, glancing at me, the youngest, "the first order of business is mice. The traps are under the sink."

While they unloaded the car I set a dozen mouse traps with cheese he had brought along just for that purpose. I put them behind the smelly couch, in smelly cabinets, up on the icebox, underneath the bunks and cots we were to sleep on.

"They seldom work," he said. "Don't much like killing the little monsters anyway. But for some reason just having the traps out seems to keep 'em in hiding. You did good, son."

That afternoon Dad and Lawrence went back to town to rent a boat, so Derald and I took a swim in the Gulf. Then Derald put on jeans (at that time he changed clothes three or four times a day) and we walked far up the beach. It was midweek and there were very few people out. A couple of fishermen battling the surf, a mother and her child, a pair of lovers. Derald was so much older that he usually spoke to me from a great distance, as if, like Lawrence, he were more an uncle than a brother.

"Thirteen, eh?" he said.

"Yeah, next week."

"That's a big one. You'll be a teenager, almost a man."

He looked at me then and a certain light entered his eyes.

"Come on," he said. "I want to show you something."

We went up into the dunes and from somewhere in his jeans he produced a pack of Marlboro's. I was astonished. Until the last year or so he had always been the good boy — Debate Club, History Club, the baseball team — a good boy with a fierce, determined depth in his eyes. He did everything with a vengeance, nothing it seemed for pleasure. If he did it he wanted to do it well and little in a boy's life came naturally to him. So he tried too hard, strained himself. Everything needed a purpose.

"Ever smoked before?" he asked.

I shook my head no.

"Well, it's time you did."

"I'm just thirteen, Derald."

"A head start then. I was almost fourteen when I started." Then his face changed and he spoke the old warning: "If you tell, I'll kill you. I mean it."

He stuck a cigarette in my mouth and lit it with a Zippo lighter that he also produced from some hidden place in his jeans. "Suck," he said. We sat there and he watched me. I could tell he had experience. He held the smoke down in his lungs and exhaled through his nose. I just puffed, like a woman my mother knew, and tried to blow smoke rings in the wind. Derald helped me, showing me how to round my lips and work my jaws, and then we just sat still, silent, like old men after a hard day's work, enjoying the scene before us: the wide and worldly roaring Gulf.

"Why do you hate Daddy?" I asked when we were up and moving again, kicking through the dunes more or less toward the trailer.

"I don't hate him."

"Well, what is it between you?"

"Nothing really."

"It must be something."

"Yeah, it's something, I guess. It's a lot of things. He wants me to be an engineer and go to Rice. He says engineers are respected and make a lot of money. He's afraid I'm going to turn out like Lawrence. More than anything he wants me to be *successful*. He wants me to have all the things they don't have."

"And you don't want to be successful?"

"I don't know what I want to be, not yet. Do you?"

He smiled like an uncle.

"And there's a girl," he said.

"Jenny?"

He nodded. "I don't know why I'm telling you this."

"What about Jenny?"

"He's afraid we're up to something and might try to get

married or something, before our time, and louse up his plans."

"Married?"

"It happens, kid, you'll see. And it's enough to drive you crazy." He stopped and looked out at the Gulf and the immense blue sky and I just watched him. It was like he was searching for something. "All I know is I want to be gone."

"You mean we'll never see you again?"

"Sure, you'll see me again, numbskull. There'll be summers and Christmas and all. I just mean out of the house."

"What's wrong with the house?"

"It's theirs."

"What's wrong with them?"

"They're them, that's all."

Confusion must have painted my face, for he did something then he had never done before without prompting from Mom or Dad for a photograph: he put his arm around me, lightly on my shoulders, and looked directly into my eyes. He was about to say something, but embarrassment caused him to glance away. The question what, what is it? was almost out of my mouth when he said, "Hey, look," and started running. "They're back."

I followed him through the dunes, trying to keep up. And then in one of the depressions I noticed he jumped, as if to avoid stepping on something, but I wasn't quick enough. That's when the strange thing happened. Just as Derald yelled, "Watch out!" I tripped and fell and something splattered.

～

"Good Lord, boy, you stink," said Lawrence.

"What is it, Dad?" asked Derald, who had run to get them. We were all four standing in the dunes looking down at the carcass.

"I don't know exactly. Kind of looks like a burro or something. I've heard there were wild burros around here."

"Must have been coyotes," said Lawrence. "Or a wolf."

"Yeah, last night or the night before," Daddy said.

The burro's belly was torn away completely and most of its neck. Flies buzzed. The stench hung in the air like a cloud and it hung on me like an overcoat. They all looked at me in fact as if I were wearing an overcoat there in the hundred-degree sunshine, as if there were something special about me all of a sudden, as if I knew something they didn't, had done something they hadn't. Even then I had read about hunters smearing the blood of a boy's first kill on his face in a rite of initiation. But I was no hunter and the blood on me was not their doing.

"Are you hurt?" my dad asked.

"No, sir."

"Well, go take a bath. Hurry. And we'll burn those clothes."

When I came outside again, Lawrence had a dinner fire going in the pit. I dropped in my tee shirt and cutoffs and we watched them burn. It was almost sunset but the sun remained a hellion in the western sky, so we sat in lawn chairs on the shady side of the trailer. On this the first night we ate well: steaks and baked potatoes, French bread and brownies. Dad and Lawrence sipped beers and Lawrence sometimes lifted his bottle of whiskey.

"Go easy on that," my dad said.

"Oh, I will, I will," said Lawrence, grinning. "Don't want to waste my old buddy."

Daddy grinned too, but kept shaking his head no whenever Lawrence offered him the bottle.

"How about you, Der?"

"No, Lawrence," said Daddy. "He's too young."

"And just how old were you, Kimo Sabe?"

Daddy grinned again. "That was a different time."

"I've tasted it," said Derald proudly, and Daddy gave him a hard but playful look of disapproval.

"A taste is one thing — "

"Oh, good Lord, Roger, the boy's about to go out and do battle with stingrays tonight, he's about to go off in a month or two and do battle with the State of Texas's finest eggheads. Why hell, he's a man in every way but one, and from what his mother tells me there's suspicion over that."

Daddy and Derald both groaned over this reference to Jenny.

"A little sip to fortify him won't hurt anything."

Again Daddy smiled. Then he said, "Gimme that bottle. And if you tell his mother, I'll kill you."

Daddy raised the bottle and took a drink and I could see by the way his body trembled that it had reached its mark and by the light in his face that the mark was a good one. He motioned to Derald to come get the bottle. Derald jumped up, took it and then stepped back. Lawrence grinned wildly, the provocateur. "Just one little one," warned Daddy. He turned up the bottle, turned it down, swallowed, and his eyes immediately went to glass. He blinked and coughed and stumbled, and the men laughed.

"Gimme that bottle," said Daddy and up it went.

Then it was Lawrence's turn again. By now the sun was down and there was a rich sheen of dying color in the low sky. The Gulf was in its evening calm and the sound of the waves came up in a peaceful rhythm. Sparks flew from the pit and their faces were bright joyous ovals in the glow of the firelight. Lawrence and Daddy joked and recalled other good times, and then somehow the bottle was in Derald's hands again and he was drinking again and I was looking on in wonder. It was a scene the likes of which I had never witnessed. It was grand. No animosity, no back talk, nothing mean at all. The electricity of brotherhood pulsed in their veins. They laughed and teased and slapped their legs, and their eyes were happy.

Lawrence had the bottle again, holding it by the neck just above the sand as if it were a great weight, and out of nowhere I heard him say, "Hey, Wayne, how about you?"

"I don't know, Larry," said Daddy. "I mean, no."

"Just a taste," cajoled Lawrence. "Come here, son."

I looked at Daddy. Lawrence looked at Daddy. Derald looked at Daddy. Daddy looked away.

"Come on, Rog," said Lawrence. "Christ, the boy killed a burro today with his bare hands. That's cause for celebration."

"Just a tiny smell, by God, and I mean it now."

The bottle was in my hands. It had such a sturdy, such an important feel, square and heavy, and I held on tightly, afraid I would drop it and ruin everything, afraid this joy would spill out of them all if the liquor spilled. I could feel their eyes on me, feel their grins. I lifted the bottle to smell. Such an odor, like something metallic and awful, a powerful fuel. I cleared my throat, swallowed, literally gulped. Then I put the bottle to my lips, waiting, savoring, a little fearful perhaps. I gulped again and then turned it up — drank the brimstone.

The men laughed and applauded, glanced at each other.

Such a feeling! Such warmth! Such a blaze of the internal lights! Now the electricity surged in my veins too.

"Wow!" I said and they laughed again.

～

So it was with light in our hearts that we set out in the car for our first night's floundering. Lawrence and Derald sang a song in Spanish. The boat on its trailer behind us banged and clattered cheerfully as Daddy drove us over the rough sandy road to the bay. Salt grass and sand dunes passed in the headlights and at one point we stunned an animal beside the road, its eyes fiery green dots. "A coon," Daddy said.

"Or a killer bobcat," Lawrence put in and he glanced back at me. Derald, beside me, sniggered and poked my ribs and I poked him back. "Hey now," he said. "Easy."

We were all alone at the boat launch, which was nothing but a jagged slab of cement at the end of the road. The night was so dark, the human touch so frail here, that Lawrence had to light a lantern before we could see what we were doing. It took him quite a while and they giggled over it. Way off, it must have been miles across the bay, gleamed one yellow speck of light.

The boat was barely large enough for the four of us and all our gear. The lantern hissed, the little Evinrude sputtered and growled and moved us forward slowly along the bank. Dad kept saying that in this bay was the best floundering in all the world, but only I paid him any attention. Derald and Lawrence were still swigging from the bottle and cutting up, and Daddy had to tell them to calm down, to hush.

"Okay, Rog," said Lawrence. "He's right, Der, you're going to scare off all the fish. And all the stingrays too." They looked at me and couldn't hide their mirth. "You know, I hear tell those things get as big as this boat."

"Why, I hear," said Derald. "I hear that they especially love to devour small boys."

"After stinging them to death first, of course."

"And you know what they do with them then?"

"That's enough," said Daddy, but he was grinning too, and Derald and Lawrence broke out laughing.

This was a serious concern to me, for in all his explanations Daddy had stressed the "safety factor." The outline of a stingray, he mentioned many times, burrowed down in the silty mud at the bottom of the bay, looks just like a flounder. And if you gig one by mistake it can tear you alive and fill you full of its poison before you have a chance to get away. I had been stung by a jellyfish once and knew the pain of such an outrage. This, though, was the challenge of the thing, he said, not to be taken lightly, this the reason for doing it. You had to be exact, you had to be careful and you had to do it alone, after midnight.

My waders filled with water as soon as they put me over the side, when I stumbled in the sucking mud and almost fell. Daddy handed me my lantern and gaff. He had rigged a rope to the handle of my net so I could tie it around my waist, not let it get away.

"You work this area right here," he said.

"Yessir."

"And don't wander off. Stay close to the shore, in the shallows. We're going to fan out and work the next two coves. We'll be back for you in three hours." He looked at me closely over the gunwale. "Remember everything I told you, son."

"Yessir."

"It's a slow, painful death," murmured Lawrence, his smirking face a pale leering disc in the lantern light.

"Hush," said Daddy. Then he cranked her up. I heard their loud voices talking and laughing over the chug of the engine for a good five minutes as the boat took them away. . . .

I looked down for the first time, peered through the circle of lighted water to the bottom. I could see my boots and other things, small things, floating around down there, but nothing was clear. Minnows flashed by. I moved my foot and a billow of silt swirled up around my ankles and I wondered how I would ever see a flounder, hidden down there, who didn't want to be seen.

I decided to wade for a bit. Like a warrior I waded, spear

in hand, raised for action. I went in orderly rows along the shore, doing a section at a time. Nothing; I saw nothing. Were there flounder here? I expanded my boundaries, moved farther down the shore toward the next point. For an hour, two, three, I waded, scanning the gray-green luminous water. Until I was tired.

I was cold too, my toes chilled. Out there was only the single yellow light, so far away, nothing else. Nothing above the water, nothing below it. Only me and my lantern. Perhaps it was time; perhaps if I looked hard enough I would see *their* light. It would grow brighter, coming for me, and they would raise their heavy stringers crowded with flounder and they would tease me good-naturedly, saying there's always tomorrow.

Something touched my leg, or I thought something did. I flinched but my boots were held fast in the mud. I raised my lantern, peered into the water, and there it was. My flounder in its hiding place. Two feet away. How had I missed it? And a big sucker too. Or maybe not. Was it a flounder? I looked closely, looked for the oval shape in the silt, the point of eye, a flicker of movement. Yes — perhaps. I looked for the stingray's telltale sign: the string-like indention in the mud behind the fishy tail. But where was the tail? Was that it? Must be. . . .

Do it!

I lunged, with power, but I missed. Just barely I missed, and it came up out of the silt so fast and furious that it must have had engines. It struck me on the rubber legs and flitted around my thighs. All of this in a second, maybe two. I swung back to get out of its way and tried to run. But my boots!

Backwards I toppled like a felled tree, and I thrashed. The brine stung my eyes and my hands sank into the muck on the bottom. Everything was dark when I struggled to my feet. The lantern was gone; I couldn't find it anywhere. The gaff too — nowhere. I thrashed some more, to be frightening this time, and then I raced for the shore, kicking through the water, panting for air.

So that was it; the thing was finished.

Where was I? It felt good to sit down, I was so tired, but what was I sitting on? And what might be lurking in the brush behind me? Killer bobcat? Don't think about it, I told myself.

Think about this: what has happened? They would laugh for sure now. No flounder, and all my gear lost; I was alone, wet, cold, frightened. Yes, they would laugh, but only if they found me. And how would they find me without my lantern's beacon to guide them to me through the darkness?

The sky was just beginning to pale when I heard the boat's motor and woke to see it a hundred yards off shore. My exhaustion had proved stronger than my fear and I had fallen asleep there in the sand.

Daddy yelled, "Wa-ayne," as if I were far away.

I waved and yelled and splashed into the water.

"Where have you been, son?" he wanted to know as I waded toward the boat.

He didn't look good. His face was haggard and angry, his cap crooked on his head. Lawrence didn't look any better. One of his shirt sleeves had been ripped from its shoulder and his hair was wild. He sat at the bow and gazed at me as if I were a suspicious stranger approaching the boat. I didn't see Derald until I was alongside. He was lying in the bottom, curled up asleep and as wet as I was. He smelled of vomit and looked the worst of all. Floating in the bilge under Daddy's seat was a seriously wounded soldier, Mr. Jack Daniel. There were no flounder hanging from stringers, no proof they had even entered the water.

Something awful had happened out there in the darkness — an argument, a fight, maybe more — and I could tell they were still suffering from the mystery of it, the hurt of it.

I put up my hands for help getting into the boat. Daddy and Lawrence both moved toward me, but Daddy stopped him.

"Don't, Larry, don't you touch him. I'll do it myself."

"Fine with me, Rog."

"Just stay where you are, you hear me."

"Shut up, Rog, would you?"

"You're not getting your hands on this one."

"Christ, Rog."

"Christ yourself," said Daddy.

He pulled me in and covered me with his flannel shirt. I explained what had happened to me in the night — how I'd had one, a big one, how I'd done battle with it, a flounder or a stingray, I didn't know which, and how I'd put up a good fight — and I told it all in a way to let them know how brave I had been. But it was mostly for myself. Neither of them laughed or smiled, neither of them spoke; they weren't interested. Their thoughts were tangled and far away, submerged in bitterness. At that moment I longed for the night again, as I long for it still: that special happiness around the fire, that electric pulse of friendship that Mr. Daniel in the glory of his gift had ignited for us. I looked at their faces — harsh and bewildered yet tinged with sad regret — and I saw then what grave difficulties awaited me as a man.

"You're not hurt then?" Daddy asked.

"No, sir," I said. I picked the bottle out of the bilge and held it in my lap, held it close like a promise.

He cranked the engine, turned us around and we set out for the boat launch, The Fish Camp and then the long drive home. We went in silence all the way. It was a mean, greedy kind of silence, and it lasted for years and years.

THE
UNYIELDING
SILENCE

Carla Acres, her small stout body covered in denim and her feet in rough-out boots, stood in the doorway of the room twisting her hands and gazing at the old man lying in the bed. He was sleeping now, thank goodness, but his scratchy breathing, catching and starting, told of a pain that no pill could ease and an exhaustion that only death would release him of. He shouldn't have come here, though she understood why he had and even sympathized with him. It would mean a battle when Warren found out. And how would she tell him when he called; how would she tell him that his father was there, sleeping in the house?

The hallway was dark after she closed his door, so she made her way quickly to the kitchen, always so cold under its high ceiling. With a match she lit the oven and stood before it to warm herself, thinking of supper alone and of what she would say to Warren when he called. She would have to go slowly.

Into a pan she poured her evening soup and set it on the low burner. There, outside the window, loomed the enormous listing barn, illuminated in wavy patches by the mercury light on its pole, up among the trees. She stood still, blinking, wondering, and then, as if something had grabbed her and pulled her out the door, she took her coat from the wall rack and hurried into the night — across the frozen yard, through the gate and into the barn, cavernous and harsh-smelling. Old Velvet, her belly swollen, about to foal at any time, whinnied deeply and turned once in her stall as Carla approached cautiously, not to frighten her. She had been nervous and fidgety at feeding time and stared at Carla as if confused by something, wanting an explanation.

"I know, girl," she said falsely, hearing the lie, for she knew nothing of the suffering of motherhood. "It won't be long."

Lady Blue and Buster in their stalls, necks low and stretched over the rails, watched her with concerned, absurdly grave expressions on their long haughty faces and even the cows, chewing and twitching, had gathered in the corner of their shed to be in attendance. What if her time arrived too soon? She had heard the vet was up near Trinity on a bad case that might keep him till morning, and not a single neighbor to rely on. What would she do? Wouldn't it be a shame to lose this one, being registered and all, so valuable. She wished Warren were home, he would know. Such a good man, a proud man, her Warren, with hands that could build or fix anything, hands with a gentle touch.

It was his gentle nature that had first attracted her to him back when she was still at the college over in

Huntsville and he was working there in town, before he had asked her to give up the life she had expected, to come live with him on the land. His forty acres. Twelve years now and still each month they held their breath till payday. This work he did for Mr. Hudson that took him away at least one week in five he did to meet the bills, and he did it well. For he too was educated in certain matters, matters having to do with machinery and equipment and the mysteries of chemicals that can transform a building made of wood and iron into a gigantic icebox. No, it wasn't the life she had expected, but she wouldn't change it: not the work, not the worries, not the frigid mornings in the old drafty house, not Warren's moods, not even the rank odors of life and death and decay which were a natural part of a place like this. It was all fine with her. They were a pair for life, she and Warren.

Velvet nuzzled her as if to wake her from a dream and she remembered her other responsibilities.

"Just hold on, girl," she said. "Hold tight."

Outside, in a drizzling rain now, the dogs collected around her for the return trip to the house and this time — it was so cold! — she allowed them to follow her into the kitchen. All but that limping mongrel who'd been hanging around despite her curses and hurled rocks. "Go on!" she snapped and closed the door. The four of them sat in a pack, licking, scratching, sneezing.

She peeked in on Mr. Acres but saw no change. Why here; why did he come here? There was something terrible between them, her husband and his father, had been for years, and what an awful chill it brought. She would have to take up for him, the old man, and everything would be difficult then for however long it lasted. And didn't they have trouble enough as it was?

In the kitchen, resting finally, warm finally in her place

at the table, she was just raising the first spoonful of noodles to her lips when the phone rang causing her to spill it.

The operator made the collect connection. "Go ahead. . . ."

"Hey, gal." He sounded so happy. "Guess what?"

"What?"

"Be home tomorrow," he said. "And all weekend too."

The idea of saying it out loud seemed to set him off. He talked for a long time about how his work had gone and then went on with questions about the mail and the weather and the animals and giving her advice about caring for Old Velvet on such a raw night. He was excited and glad for the chance to talk to her and she could tell in the things he said and the way he said them that he loved her and wanted like Holy Hell, as he would put it, to be with her just then. It sickened her to have to spoil it.

"Warren," she said to prepare him but he didn't respond and so she said again, "Warren?" as if calling out in the night.

"What is it, Carla?" His voice was light and expectant.

"It's about your father," she said.

II

Sunup was still an hour away when Warren Acres checked out of the motel in Texarkana and headed south on U.S. 59 hoping to make Huntsville and home by lunchtime. The rain had let up in the night and the last of the stars had had a chance to make an appearance, like a thousand gleaming eyes in a black sky so clear and immense it hurt even to glance up at it.

By the time he reached Marshall there was enough of a glow in the east that he could switch off his headlights and quit worrying about every bridge he came to and whether he was going to find himself spinning and sliding

and ending up in the bottom of a creek bed somewhere.
The fierce wind battered the old Ford and moaned like a
demon, slipping in through the wings. A snapping, beauty
of a day but so God-awful cold that his knee wouldn't stop
tingling and the hair on his neck pricked him like pins.

*So the old man's come home, has he. Wants us to make him
a place, like a bed for an old dog that shows up just to die on
your front porch, or under it, and leaving you with the nasty
business of digging the hole to put him in. Well, why should
we, why should we bother with him? He's never much bothered
with us. Gone for thirteen years and showing up just when
he needs something, money usually or a hot meal from Carla,
and then taking off again in the middle of the night. Why, he
couldn't even be found to attend his only son's wedding, and in
his own house that he built with his own hands. He wouldn't
have come anyway, with Mother there, but it was the idea of
it. He killed her sure enough with his restless ways and his
liquor and then running off with that old gal, Shirley was her
name, living with her in that stinking trailer house in that stinking town out there in that stinking desert where nothing'll grow
but cholla cactus.*

*And so now she's gone too, and his time up, the cancer eat-
ing him alive, and he wants us to care for him. And Carla,
with a tender heart for animals, even the human kind, anything
in pain, and Carla taking up for him. He's got a right, sure, it
was his place — his and Mother's, mind you — his land, his
house, his trees, his debts too, that we took. But it's ours now,
ours, free and clear, no matter where it came from. You work a
place eleven years and it ought to be yours and it ought to be up
to you who can die on it and who can't. It was his, sure, it
was, and maybe he's got a right. . . . Better get there, better
get home.*

He recalled what Carla had said the night before and
how her voice on the line went low and deep so the old

man wouldn't hear what she said, not that he could have heard much with one ear smashed and silent and the other so weak that you had to holler at him to get his attention. "But he's your father."

And Warren came back: "I don't care, I don't care if he's my patron saint, I won't have him. Not in our house."

"It's his house too."

"No sir, not anymore."

"And just what is he to do?"

"There's Becky. She's his sister, let her take care of him."

"But Warren, that old lady couldn't care for a kitten, she's so weak and senile, and with a bad hip and that Billy of hers still in the house at the age of fifty."

"Then let him go to the poorhouse."

"Warren!"

"I don't see what's wrong with the Veteran's Hospital down in Houston, that's what it's there for."

"But Warren — "

"Don't 'But Warren' me."

"But Warren," she said and he let her do it. "Is that where I should take you when the time comes?"

He thought about this for a moment, thought of the way it was with men like them, how they had both gone to their wars and how they had both spent their time in Army hospitals, twenty-five years apart, and how they both received their disability checks each month, the pittance that at least kept them from starving, and how the only thing for men such as them was to end their days among the lonely and ragged within the high inhuman walls of a government institution. And he said, "Yes."

"No, and you know better too," she said. "He doesn't want to die in a hospital."

How was he to argue with her? After another period of

silence she mentioned the long-distance charges they were piling up and said they'd better talk about this when he got home.

"I don't want him there."

She didn't answer.

"I'll throw him out," said Warren. "After I have my say."

"Please be careful," said Carla.

He waited, stewing, then muttered, "You too."

"Love you," she said.

"Yes," he said, though he wished now that he had said more.

He was just outside Lufkin, having made better time than he'd expected, crossing the Angelina River bridge, his thoughts already at the house, his boot firm on the pedal. He felt no surprise or shock, only anger over the delay it would cause, when, reaching pavement again, in a deep and long stretch of shade, the truck veered sharply to the left as if under its own control and then spun around on a patch of ice. The tailgate struck the ditch embankment. The impact jostled him but nothing was hurt.

"Why'd you come back?" he said after a moment of stillness.

Then he opened the door and stepped out, into the mud.

III

It was after noon before Warren found a farmer willing to pull him out with his tractor for twenty dollars. The old guy reminded him of his father, with bandy legs in faded jeans and a waist as small as it was the day he became a man, and a dirty mule skinner jacket with corduroy on the collar, and a straw hat with its brim rolled crudely into a funnel at the front, and tennis shoes on his feet, and a cigarette in his mouth. He was still agile, hooking up the chain, but bent and slow.

"You just stand back there, son," the old guy hollered, smiling at Warren from his noisy tractor, the cigarette hanging off his lip. It was then that Warren noticed the rotten brown teeth and the rotten brown cancer splotches on his cheeks and noticed how he even sounded like his father.

"Now you're set, sure enough," he said when Warren handed him the twenty and thanked him. "Happier'n a dead pig in sunshine, I'd bet." He grinned impudently. "Go easy now," he yelled, waving, and started off slowly down the highway.

Chunks of mud rattled against the wheel wells of the truck. Even at two o'clock the sun was low in the southern sky, glaring at him through the windshield, but the ice was gone from the warming road. The pines along the road swayed like dancers in the wind. Warren was colder in his bones than he'd been in years.

He would be lucky now to make it home by dark. Again he found himself driving faster than he should; he wanted to get there. He had things to do, and to say. He had a lot to say. He wanted to tell him one last time what he thought of him and let him know that he would have to pay for the way he had lived and what he had done. Yes, he had a lot to say. And in the morning Warren would drive him to the hospital in Houston and walk him inside and leave him there, and he would be through with it then.

Too bad, really, the way things turned out. They had been close when he was young, a hard-edged older man and his big boy. He would take Warren to town on his errands and he would heft him onto the counter and the other men would tease the boy and the women would smile. Later, when he was older, they hunted together and played pitch in the yard, and later still, in his youth, there were the Friday night football games at the high school and he remembered even now the sound of his father's voice from the grandstand, yelling the loudest, laughing and smiling afterwards, making a fool of himself in front of the others. And there was the night he took the young man to the Tarry Awhile Tavern for the first time and set him down with his first ever taste of whiskey. Warren remembered how tenderly his father had stood over him later alongside the road home, holding him by the neck as Warren retched into the weeds, saying, "That's it, get it all out." And there was, later still, the firm manly handshake and the wet eyes on the day Warren, dressed in his uniform, left for the war, and then the short misspelled letters of encouragement and gossip that he received once a week for three years. He learned even later that his father wrote those letters, never dated, while his mother was away at church on Sunday mornings.

So what had happened? It was true they had never gotten along — his father, the local rascal, and his mother, the stern-faced Baptist who quoted scriptures and prayed for his soul — but something had changed by the time Warren was home again. There was hatred between them and they all fought about it. Warren knocked him down once after parrying his weak blows and he refused to be helped up. He took his revenge on Warren's mother and there was another fight, mostly shouts and the slamming of doors, and Warren moved to town, and then everything went to hell.

"It's yours," he said one day, meaning the land and the house. He had come into Huntsville where Warren was working then, just to see him. He was dressed up and his own truck was packed with two suitcases, a few boxes in the back. "Tend it for your mother and it's yours when she's gone, as far as I'm concerned."

"You bastard," said Warren.

"You don't understand this," he said.

"I understand you're a bastard."

His father smiled sadly and nodded his head and it was many years before Warren saw him again.

Finally, Huntsville. The house wasn't far now. It was late afternoon and the clouds were back, low and dark. From what he could tell it was getting even colder. Might even snow, the radio said. He hated to go home without something for Carla but he was in such a hurry. . . . At a service station he stopped to fill up the truck on Mr. Hudson's money and on the counter sat some samplers of chocolate-covered cherries. She loved those things. He bought a box; at least he'd have something.

There were two strange trucks in the yard. Coming in the long rutted drive toward the house he recognized one of them. Dr. Sweeney, here to see about Old Velvet. The other was brand new, a fancy job with chrome wheels, parked next to his father's Dodge. Carla, alone, was waiting for him on the porch.

"Where have you been?" she said, pulling the lapels of her heavy coat tight against her chest. "I've been worried to death."

He mentioned the accident, calling it "very minor," and asked her what in the name of reason she was doing out there in the cold. "Just waiting," she said, clapping her gloved hands, and he limped to the bottom of the steps gazing up at her. She looked like the best thing he had ever seen in his life, the essence of warmth, but he knew the look she was offering was meant to put him on his guard. He handed her the box of chocolates, saying, "For you," and she showed him a quick smile before putting it away in her deep pocket. Carla drew him to her then and they sat down together, hands linked in her lap.

"Warren," she said and he cocked his head.

"Warren." It was a warning to prepare himself. "He died this afternoon, just awhile ago. The doctor's in there with him now."

IV

Sometime in the night Warren got out of bed and went into the room where his father had died. The room was chilly, and even chillier when he switched on the bedside lamp, its glow pale and blue. This had been his room when he was a boy and it still held the furniture his parents had bought second-hand or made for him. The narrow chest of drawers and the boy's desk in the corner with its ladder-back chair and the oval rug on the floorboards and the bed with the bookcase headboard in which rested Carla's childhood collection of rag dolls. At first they had hoped this room would be lived in by their own children, but then, over time, it became known as the guest room, though they seldom had guests.

In the corner sat his father's old-fashioned suitcase. Draped over the chair were the clothes he was wearing when he arrived the day before, "coughing like a consumptive and all but falling out of the truck when he opened the door," as Carla had put it. There were his jeans and a western shirt and a corduroy jacket with a cheap furry collar. On the floor sat his boots, the uppers lying on their sides like the wings of a bird. Carla had put out his "personal items" on a towel atop the bureau. A razor and a soap mug with a faded etching of an old sailing ship on the side and a pocket comb stuck into the bristles of a brush. He had always been meticulous about his hair, even toward the end when there was precious little of it left, thin and pearly. He found a ring, a simple gold band, worn smooth, and he wondered if it had been from his mother or from Shirley, the other one.

He had looked quite handsome in death, his skin clear but for the splotches and his jaw set against his chest and his eyes closed as if in prayer. Warren remembered, standing above the bed, staring down at the Mexican blanket Carla had covered it with after the doctor had signed the death certificate and the undertaker's son had come and gone with the body. Carla had combed his hair for him and there was a look of — well, what? Dignity, perhaps? Serenity? The way the dead always look once they've been fussed over and prepared by the living.

"I'm sorry you died," Warren said out loud, his voice a separate presence in the room.

Then Carla was standing in the doorway. Her hair was down and the hem of her robe lay on the floor around her hidden feet.

"He had wanted very badly to see you again," she said.

She took a seat on the bed, patted the place beside her as an invitation, but he turned away. He parted the curtains and looked out at the snow falling gently, whispering gently, and the eerie gray sheen of the weighty clouds. White patches were already forming on the ground between the trees and on the tops of the fence posts. It had not snowed in that part of Texas in many years and he knew it would be all the talk that day.

"What else did he tell you?" Warren asked and glanced at her. He saw that Jasper, the only one of the dogs she allowed to sleep with them, had roused himself and come in to see. He was resting against her leg as she absently rubbed his white chin.

"He was disappointed that you weren't here when he arrived," she said with a worried look. "He told me to tell you he loved you and missed you and hoped you'd understand him."

He snorted through his nose, a sound of mockery, derision.

"He told me to tell you that your peach trees were going to need more pruning in February and to be sure to transplant the blackberry shoots at the same time."

Again he snorted, scoffing, ridiculing, dismissing.

"He was worried about our little orchard?"

"Yes, he was," she said. "He sat at that window and looked out at it for a long time. How he could see it, I don't know, he was so blind, and he wouldn't bother with his glasses once he got out of the truck. Oh, and he said to be sure and separate Old Velvet and the little one from the other horses for a while."

"I know that," Warren said. "Sweeney and I talked about it, and besides I already knew that."

"He wanted to feel useful, that's all. He knew how much she means to you, and this new one, too, being a purebred. That's all he had to leave you with, he said, advice and this house."

He gave her a severe glance to let her know that he didn't like going into that, that they had settled that piece of old business long ago and he would never see it her way, or his.

"Warren?" she said. He let the curtains go but didn't turn to listen. "Warren," she said. "He wanted me to ask you a favor. It was very important to him. I was going to wait till tomorrow."

She hesitated until he said, "Well?"

"He wanted . . . why, you know what he wanted. He wanted you to bury him here, on the property, next to your mother."

There was a long adamant silence during which only

the happy panting of the dog could be heard and the almost-sound of the whispering snow. Warren said, "I figured as much.

"But I won't do it, you know. He gave up all his rights here, to this place and to her both, and I won't do it, I won't."

"That's so spiteful, Warren, not to forgive. It seems wrong."

"Spite or revenge or whatever you want to call it — that doesn't matter. I won't do it, wrong or right."

"Well, and just what would we do then?"

"I'll think of something."

"I'm not sure we have even enough money to buy him a decent suit or a casket, much less a plot in the cemetery. He left nothing, you know, but thirty-two dollars in his wallet and some change there in the bureau. What will we do with him?"

"I'll think of something," he said again and the tone of his voice made it clear that this was the end of it for now. Again the unyielding silence, only the sound of the dog snuffling after Carla's house shoe, trying gently to remove it from her foot with his mouth, and Carla's murmur, "No, no."

V

Warren was not in the house when Carla woke the next day. It was almost seven and this was to be expected but she could tell he hadn't come back to bed that night. Out in the barn she found him, sitting on a wheelbarrow in front of Old Velvet's stall.

"Ain't he a beaut," Warren said of the colt. "Just like his mama." His breath was thick and frosty and smelled of liquor.

It was all understandable. Carla smiled and took his hand.

"Dr. Sweeney was really pleased with the way it went. Everything was fine, he said. A prizewinner, he called him."

Carla watched as Warren stepped into the large stall and maneuvered between the mare and the colt and then she watched as he stood there brushing Velvet and talking to her softly. She was a stocky carrot-colored sorrel they had admired for many years before saving the money to buy her. Back then they would stop on the road in front of the Jones place and pet her over the fence, and Mr. Jones would wave and call, "She's yours whenever you want her. I'm saving her for you." It had been two years more before they raised the money to breed her with Pay Dirt, the big quarter horse stud that all the men in the county knew about.

"It's a pleasure to watch you with her like that," Carla said. "She's so easy with you, and you with her."

"We got a way with each other, that's for sure," he said and she saw that his eyes were shining when he turned into the light.

"Well now," she said. "How about some breakfast?"

"That's a good idea," he said without looking at her.

She would wait until he had a hot meal in his stomach before bringing up the matter of his father again. They would have to decide something and she thought she knew him well enough to know that he had been speaking through grief and exhaustion the night before, that he would feel differently now, in the daylight, and such a tender day, soft blue above sharp white. As she crunched across the patchy snow in the yard she glanced off through the trees beyond the leafless orchard at what Warren called the family plot. The short chain-link fence glistened with icicles and a peak of powdery snow lay on his mother's gravestone.

It was Mr. Hudson's truck coming through the gate. She waved to him from the porch when he stopped and got out on the drive, and he waved back warmly before walking off toward the barn. He was a short round man with a shaggy moustache who lived on a beautiful ranch about five miles away. He liked Warren and respected his opinions and his work and he had always treated her husband as something of a son, for he too had begun life poor and had made his mark in business with labor and loyalty. They talked on the telephone at least once each day, often before sunrise, and he often came by just to get away from his huge household.

Mr. Hudson leaned against the fence. Then she saw that Warren had brought Old Velvet out of her stall and was tying her to a fence rail. Soon he came out with the colt who stood shakily next to his mother, nuzzling her underside, and then Warren crawled through the fence to stand beside Mr. Hudson. Come to admire and console, she said to herself and then went inside.

The sausage was still sizzling when Carla called the men in for breakfast. Their boots thundered on the back porch as they stomped away the snow and the sound of it was reassuring to her.

Mr. Hudson smiled at her and shook her hand politely, saying, "Carla, how the hay are you?" in his high friendly voice, as he did every time they met. He offered no condolence.

"Have a seat, Mr. Hudson," she said and started putting the platters of food on the table. The room was warm and fragrant.

"Carla, I wish you'd talk him out of it," said Mr. Hudson in a glad, teasing way. It was obvious he didn't know.

She glanced at Warren, who was sullen-seeming and wouldn't look up at her. She said, smiling as if at a joke,

"What's that, Mr. Hudson?" and took her own seat between the men.

"The horses!" he said but he was really speaking to Warren. "It seems a real shame selling them. Now, I'd be a damn fool not to buy them, even at three-thousand, and I've wanted Old Velvet for years, but it docs seem a damn shame. I know there's no changing his mind once it's made up and I'm sure y'all have your own reasons, but still — "

"Business is business, Mr. Hudson, as you always say."

This was Warren speaking and the sound of his voice saddened her, the things being said astonished her. There was an emptiness in her heart, a silence, as Mr. Hudson went on talking gladly about the horses and filling his plate with food. She understood now, though she would never truly understand it, and she looked at her husband to question him: his eyes, so much like his mother's just then, dark and wounded, hooded with bitter secrets, refused again to meet her gaze. She wouldn't have thought him capable of this, of going so far to get his revenge. She dared not say anything, for he would never forgive such disloyalty, and besides everybody would know soon enough. It was wrong.

Carla stared at him trying to attract his eyes. Only once did they glance at her — a quick shift and a shift away, without contact — and she realized even then, with fear, that this was how they would be with each other for a long, long time.

MOTHER'S
THIMBLES

There are twenty-three, now twenty-four thimbles on the arm of my lawn chair. I adjust the position of one in the middle — the one with the image of Mount Rushmore etched into it — so they line up perfectly. The thimbles were all that Mother left me when she died. I don't know why she thought I'd want them. An only child I was, though, and I guess she wanted me to have something of hers. Now I pull them out of the old sewing cabinet whenever I'm home, take a look, feel the cool of metal and porcelain on my fingers.

Pop moves in his chair. He's been quiet for half an hour, but now he says, "She loved those things," and I nod. We look at each other. I shrug, uncertain what he wants with his drooping, sad eyes, if he wants me to say something. But he says, "She really loved those things," and our eyes turn away, go searching for something that we cannot find in the other one's face.

Beyond the yard and the chain-link fence, way out on that damn treeless Wyoming horizon, a pump jack is working against the sunset. Its big horse head bobs up slowly and then dips again. I scan the line where the yellow field touches the pale sky, but there is nothing: no bushes, no cacti, very little grass. Why he settled here I'll never know. The place is so high and open and lonely that it makes me feel like an ant when I visit. This is country that takes your heart out and throws it away as soon as you cross the border. Maybe that's why he came here. Maybe he needed his heart to be thrown away when Mom died. He's healthy. He says the doctors give him ten, maybe twenty years to live. Imagine being heartbroken for twenty years.

I glance at him, and he must sense my interest. He says, "It's sure been good having you, Jimbo."

"Yeah, Pop, it's been good. Thanks for putting me up."

"Any time," he says. "Any time."

His expression goes intense again and I can see that he is concentrating, watching the changing light in the sky. Weather permitting, he sits out here every evening. Sometimes, when I sit with him, I feel like an intruder, an unwanted presence, an irritating charge in the atmosphere that interferes with his thoughts. He told me once that the evening clouds above Wyoming help him evoke the image of Mom, of Katty as he called her, better than any clouds anywhere. And he's been around. Tonight the colors run together, gray and purple, a wash of amber angling through it, holding everything together like a seam.

I've been here a week, sleeping in my old bed, eating his hotcakes in the morning, drinking his "for-guests-only" bourbon at night. He assumes I'm leaving in a day or two. In the past I've stayed only a few days at a time, twice at

Christmas, once at Easter, always with Jackie, my wife. But this time it's different. I don't know when I'm leaving. No job to go to, and no Jackie now. He doesn't know about that. I told him she had to work and couldn't make the trip. At night I pull the phone into the bedroom and fake long-distance calls to her. I do it for him. I know he listens, and he would wonder if I did nothing.

Pop says, as if he knows what I'm thinking about, "Too bad Jackie's not with you. We could take a day and run over to Mount Rushmore, show her the faces." My elbow flinches, bumps the thimbles and one of them falls to the ground, bounces, lights on a tuft of his neatly trimmed grass.

∼

In the morning we go to town. It's a short ride; he lives in a subdivision of fifteen or twenty houses owned by people in the oil and gas business, the few guys still trying it around here, and a community of retirees like himself. He has friends; they get together after church and for Spades on Friday nights and for coffee at the Old Mill Cafe on Custer Street.

He directs his pickup into a parking place at the curb in front of the cafe. "Why don't you go on in," he says. "I've got an errand to run. Won't be long." I watch him as he walks away along the high-curbed sidewalk. His bald spot and wispy gray hair shine above his shoulders; his strides are short, purposeful, but erratic, as if he has to think about each step.

I sit at a booth in the corner. It's an old place, like the town, with glass-enclosed pie stands on the counter and the stuffed heads of game animals on the walls. But the waitress is pretty and she smiles for me, a genuine smile. She puts down water, a paper napkin and Army surplus silverware. I look up. She is smiling again in a direct, familiar way, and it's then that I realize I know her. "Hello, Jimbo," she says, but I can't recall her name until she helps: "Charlene. Remember?"

"Char-lene," I say, tapping my forehead. High school; we'd known each other in Houston. "What are you doing here?"

"That's what I was going to ask you."

She sits across from me and we talk for a while as old acquaintances do when they meet by chance at odd places in the world, and under odd circumstances, and I learn that she is in Newton, Wyoming, for much the same reason I am. An aunt and uncle are here, she needed a place and they took her in, found her this job. She says, "It's just temporary, until I figure things out."

"Sure, I know. Me, too."

"I heard — it's been years now — I heard you'd married."

I nod, but say nothing, indicate nothing of the trouble. "Any kids?"

I shake my head no, and she says, "Me either. I'm divorced. You probably didn't even know I was married."

"It figures. I mean, we were all raised to get married."

"I'm over it, though," she says as if she didn't hear me.

I say, "Here's Pop," and she stands up in a hurry, brushes down her apron. I introduce them, explain briefly, and she says that she needs to get back to work. "I'll give you a minute."

Right off he says, "Still got the old attraction, eh Jimbo. The easy ones always come running." He has teased me about this ever since the first time he discovered I'd been with a girl and Mother insisted that he instruct me in the ways of nature. But he's never been one to talk frankly about "intimate relations" and even at his age he blushes over the topic. Teasing me is how he compensates, though it ended mostly when I married Jackie and moved to Oklahoma. Now he says, "Remember that gal — " but I cut him off. "Don't, huh. Charlene's not like that."

"You're right," he says quickly, charitably, his face going red. "And it's unfair to Jackie, you know. Even among the guys."

Charlene is back, ready to take our order.

~

The wind has shifted and this evening I can hear the pump jack working. Like an animal caught in a trap, it moans as it struggles. Pop is full of questions. He wants to know how the job is going; I tell him fine. And Jackie, how's her work? Fine. He goes on. Are we getting along all right? I avoid him, say, "As well as can be expected," but he picks up something in my voice.

"What is it? Come on, you can tell me."

"It's nothing, Pop."

We stare at the clouds, a brilliant lavender.

"You got to work at a marriage, you know that, Jimbo? Your mother and I, we worked every day for thirty-six years, and I wouldn't have traded her for anything. A man, a woman, they're meant to be together — and I mean for life. It's natural that way. That's the way nature meant it, and the home you make is sacred."

I groan, and he looks over from his lawn chair.

"Go ahead, make fun of your old man, but I'm telling you it is. You protect that home with everything you've got. With your life, if need be. A good woman needs pro-tecting."

I sigh, and he must take it wrong.

"That's right, you little — " He stops, but then: "You laugh, go ahead, but do you know that I couldn't even imagine taking another woman into my home. Your moth-er will always be there, and I wouldn't dream of muddying her good memory. You should think about that, Jimbo. Don't risk it."

"That's enough, *huh!*" I don't really mean the emphasis, but it touches something inside him and we stare at each other in a mild anger until it's obvious one of us has to speak or move. So he stands up and slogs through the grass to the fence at the back of his lot. He holds onto the fence, looks out at the horizon, and soon I see his head dip, rise, dip again. His big shoulders heave. I think he is crying. And it's my fault. But there's nothing I can do, so I go inside to leave him to himself. I wander through the house until I come to the sewing cabinet.

Sitting on the cabinet is a picture of Mother in a cheap golden frame. I've seen it a hundred times, but I pick it up anyway. It's a studio shot from during the war, the big war, "My war," he likes to say. They had just been married, though it would be more than a year before he was mustered out in '46 and almost eight before I entered their lives. Mother is beautiful against the dark background, and there is something of a halo around her hair, her face, which is smooth, molded, no sharp angles, no disturbing lines. In her eyes is hope. She is gazing up, and the photographer's light sparkles in her eyelashes. This, and I can see it, this must be what he finds in the clouds.

I take out the thimbles, place each one on my pinky to examine it and then line them up in groups of five along the edge of the cabinet. They are like little hands reaching up to me.

⌒

Later, after Pop's in bed, I go back to the Old Mill Cafe.

Charlene is still there, sitting at the counter, eating dinner.

"Oh, hi," she says. "I just got off. Have you had supper?"

I tell her yes, but sit on the stool beside her and we talk. At first we talk about Newton, how small it is, how little there is to do and how the country round about is nothing if it's not dry and hot and boring. I tell her that Pop and I take a lot of naps and she tells me that she has had the time to make herself "an entire new wardrobe." Gradually we get into history, our history, and we talk about the people and things we knew in high school, of old sweethearts and old enemies, of the year we graduated and dispersed. Charlene and I had been close enough to date a few times, talk occasionally on the phone, sign each other's pictures in the yearbook. I remember what I wrote: "Wish we'd gotten to know each other better. But, alas, maybe someday." The "alas" embarrasses me now and I hope she has forgotten it.

"Weren't you in the war?" she says and I nod. "So was John, my husband. He was a Captain."

"I was a private. Private First Class. I was drafted."

She takes her last bite, then I tell her, very abruptly, "My wife and I have split up," and she stares at me with brown eyes so dark and intuitive they seem almost black. They are nice eyes, encouraging eyes. "I wanted you to know, for some reason."

"I sort of thought so," she says. "I could tell, somehow."

Slowly a smile brightens her face until we are both smiling and then grinning and then, very nearly, laughing.

"Listen," I say. "Is there some place we could get a beer?"

~

Above the entrance to the Cowboy Bar, hanging per-

pendicular to the brick facade, is a neon cowboy riding a
neon bronc. The cowboy's neon spurs spin when the color
of the light changes from red to white to red again. Inside
it is loud and smoky and thick with cowboys playing pool,
or dancing with cowgirls, or looking forlornly into glasses
of beer. She tells me, almost yelling over the noise of the
juke box, that every town in Wyoming has a Cowboy Bar.
"And every one of them is just like this one."

We drink, listen to the music, try to talk between songs.
I think that she wants me to ask her to dance, but I don't
and eventually I decide that she doesn't want to dance.
She doesn't seem the type — these people are kicking up
heels and cavorting wildly — with her sandals and long,
homemade skirt, her long, straight hair. I look at her face,
which is faintly illuminated by the light of a barroom can-
dle on the table, and I see, at this moment, that she is
beautiful against the dark background.

She says, raising her voice, "John loved these joints,"
and I say, after a moment's thought, "Come on, let's go."

～

The Wyoming night is soft against the skin; it is warm
and dry and somehow nurturing in the way the gentle
breeze makes me want to inhale deeply. The sky is
almost white now with stars. Once the sound of the
music fades behind us I can hear nothing but our own
footfalls on the pavement of the sidewalk. We walk
slowly but after several blocks I realize that we are very
nearly to the edge of town. At a corner we stop and she
says, "This is my street. My aunt and uncle live right
down the block."

"Do you want to go home?"

"I'm tired. Nine hours today. I'm trying to save money."

Hesitating, I gaze up at the white night sky, but then

say, "Savings is all I've got now." She looks at me like she doesn't understand, and I go on, "I'm out of work too. The oil business is slow in Oklahoma right now and I got myself laid off."

Her eyes say, I'm sorry, Jimbo, but there is nothing words can do about something like that, so we turn the corner and start toward the house a few blocks away.

I say, "I've been curious. Do you remember what you wrote in my yearbook, what you said?"

"Oh, yes: 'To thine own self be true.' It was right out of sophomore English."

"Do you remember the rest?"

"Yes." Her face brightens with wonder. "How funny. I thought about it today after you left. But it's embarrassing now."

"You said that we would meet again someday, 'in a place far away, at a time when we both would be longing for love — ' "

"Each. I said 'each,' not 'both.' But please don't go on."

"Why not? It was good."

"It was prophetic perhaps but not good. I was not a poet and I don't want to admit that I had a horrible crush on you."

We smile to ourselves and go quiet again, walking on. Soon the pavement turns to dirt and my boots kick up little tumbleweeds of dust that float around our knees, cling to our clothes. I can tell she's thinking about something, but, though I hate to intrude, I do want conversation. I say, "Spill it."

She smirks at the old phrase, says, "I was just wondering what you're going to do. I'm talking about work, or whatever."

"I've been wondering that myself. College taught me how to do one thing, but nobody's hiring geologists these days, not even around here. Maybe Alaska, though. I hear there's work up there."

"I'd like Alaska. But could you live in the cold like that?"

I say, "It seems I've been living in the cold for a long time," and she glances up, gives me a sad smile, the sort of smile that two people with nothing in the world to lose except themselves — two people like us — well, it's the sort of smile you share with each other when you're walking side by side down a dusty road in a little town called Newton, Wyoming, on a warm summer night in the middle of your life.

"What about Oklahoma?"

"No reason, really, to go back. The split's pretty wide."

Again her eyes apologize, and we keep walking, wading in the dust. Her aunt and uncle's house is brick, two bedrooms I would say by its size and configuration, with a low concrete porch and a yellow bug light out front. It's very similar to the house that Jackie and I had in Oklahoma City, but that, too, is gone now — at least for me.

Charlene says, "I'm off tomorrow. If you'd like, we could do something."

I would like, but I'm not sure this should go any further, only because I know enough to know that a man without a job has nothing but trouble to give to anybody, and I know that I should be leaving soon, going somewhere, maybe Alaska. The money I have won't last two weeks, and I can't live off Pop. But I say, "Maybe I'll drop by. We'll see."

She nods, offers me a look that says "No Pressure," and then, appearing a little embarrassed, she stands on tiptoes to kiss me. I like the kiss, hold it for just a moment, gripping her arms in my hands, remembering that it's been many, many years since I kissed lips that didn't belong to Jackie. When I let go of her I see her eyelids fluttering open — such an innocent thing. And I feel more for Charlene at this moment than I've felt for anybody in a very long time. It's the sort of thing I want to hold on to right now. It's a feeling of calm, I guess.

"So long, Jimbo," she says, and already I miss her voice.

I walk away across her aunt and uncle's lawn and turn at the street, wave to her, say, "Good night," and she says, "Good night," and again my boots are kicking up dust.

~

I'm home in ten minutes. Trying to be quiet, I let myself into the kitchen with the key Pop loaned me, then I go to my room. The room is small, just large enough for the bed and dresser he has crammed into it. My old boots slide off easily and I lie down on the bed, but then spring back up, slip into the hall and bring the phone inside. It's Jackie's number I dial, my old number, though it's another man's voice that answers.

"Oh," I say and then stutter an apology if I bothered him, but I'd like to know if my wife is home.

"Yes, certainly, yes, just a moment." I hear shuffling in the background and remember the phone is on the night-stand — must be sheets, bed clothes, naked bodies — and then it all goes silent when the guy cups the receiver. Very suddenly I hear, "Jim?"

"Yeah, it's me."

"At this hour?" I hear her say to him, "What time is it?" And then, "God, Jim, it's one-thirty."

"Twelve-thirty here, but I didn't call to talk about time."

"Well, then what? Are you hurt?"

"I want to come home."

The silence on the line is so deep and dark and far away that I wait as if to hear a pebble fall to the bottom of the Grand Canyon. I imagine her mouth open, her pale red hair a mess atop her lean, serious face, her body on its side held up by an elbow on the sheets. And I can see our bedspread all tangled about her, and the bookcase headboard with my paperbacks and her big hardback business books angled in between the clock radio and the picture of the dog. Then I imagine him. Though I've never seen him in the flesh, I can see him now: a strained, concerned, yet half-amused scowl on his face.

She says, "Look, Jim, can't we talk in the morning?"

"Why? It's simple. I want to come home."

"Let's talk in the morning."

"Why not now?"

"Because it's not morning."

"What difference does that make?" I'm getting mad, even though I know I shouldn't; it's doing me no good. "Nothing's going to change by morning."

"I have to work, Jim."

"Jackie, please, listen — " But she stops it, saying, "Jim, Jim, look — well, wait just a minute," and then he says something and she responds, and he responds, and by the time she's back on the line I've slammed the phone down. It bounces out of the cradle so I pick it up and I slam it down again, and again, until it seats itself and I can leave it alone. Then I hear it, and I turn. Pop's standing in the doorway.

For two hours we talk, sitting on the bed, him in his old flannel robe, me in my jeans and tee shirt. I explain everything and I even yell when I lay on the gritty part about the other guy and how I didn't know. Getting it out is a big relief, but there's still something churning inside me. He pats my shoulders, keeps saying, "What a shame," and shaking his head and saying, "You got to go back. You got to work it out. After six years you can't just let it burn away." Then he slips in, "This would of killed your mother," and it sends me to my feet. I stammer in frustration, "God, Jesus, damn, Pop. Why bring her into this?"

"Watch your tongue when you're talking about your mother."

"I'm not talking about her."

"Well, be careful."

We fume in silence, looking at each other, until he says, "This would of killed your mother," and he hangs his head. On go my boots and up comes his head: "Where you going?" But I don't answer and out the door I am before he can get up and follow. His voice comes to me through the house: "Go home to her, Jimbo."

~

In the truck the green lights of the dashboard are not very friendly as I drive through town and out of town and then up to the top of a hill that overlooks everything. I get out and go to the edge of the hill. Below me, spreading out for miles, are dots of light — porch lights, rig lights, car lights on the highway. They fan out from Newton like a little solar system racing away from a star. Looking hard I find Pop's neighborhood, imagine I can see his street, and then look to find the house of Charlene's aunt and uncle, but it's hidden among buildings on the far side of town. And then I remember something that seems very important.

My mother was my father's second wife. He told me the story a dozen or more years ago, just before I shipped out for the war, as if he wanted me to know in case it was the last time we saw each other. He was very solemn when he told me, embarrassed perhaps, as we had always been extremely religious people, members of a Southern congregation that shunned the divorced.

They had married the summer he graduated from high school. "We just couldn't wait, you have to see. You know how it is." And before the first year was up she gave birth to a child, a boy, "very much like you." But she was a restless girl and my father ambitious. He worked hard and was gone often for weeks at a time in the oil fields of West Texas where the really good money was to be had back then. "It seemed every time I came home there'd be a new piece of furniture in the house or she'd be wearing a new dress and there the baby'd be dragging around dirty diapers and we'd argue and yell and scream, but nothing ever changed." For two years they lived in an undercurrent of anger and lust until one day he came home and it was apparent she hadn't been alone. "I mean, a pair of the guy's drawers were right there in the bedroom. She didn't even have the decency to pick 'em up."

I recall that he told me this story as we were eating dinner one Friday night at a hot dog place near the house in Houston. Mom was still at work, doing the books at the paint store where she punched a clock for nearly three decades so they could send me to college and buy a new car every four years. When he got to the part about "she didn't have the decency to pick 'em up," he stopped chewing, stared at his plate, glanced up at me but quickly went back to his plate, and said, "We killed that boy."

They had argued — "violently, violently we argued" — and he snatched up the baby and stuffed some things into a bag and started out the door, his wife of two years following and tugging on his sleeves and grabbing at his hair, and on the landing — "we were living in a garage apartment, you see" — he turned to throw back one last good obscenity, but she was stronger than he thought and she clutched the baby's arms and refused to let go and he held onto the baby's legs and refused to let go and the baby was wailing and neighbors were out below screaming up to please hold it down or they'd call the police, and in the midst of this human scramble "something went wrong, real wrong."

He said, "I remember leaning over the bannister and literally watching that boy, my son, you've got to understand — I watched him fall, and it lasted only a split second though it seemed it lasted a very long, long time and then I saw him hit the pavement and then I saw — " He stopped. He put down his hot dog, took a drink of the soda he had been nursing and I could see that he was putting all his energy into restraining the natural emotional explosion that his body wanted to let go with.

"I was a wreck for years, you see, Jimbo. All through the war I didn't care about nothing, like I wanted to die. But then your mother came into my life — " I said, "Don't, Pop," and he didn't. He reached across the table and squeezed my arm.

When I pull myself together and shake off the nearness of the memory I am more or less overcome by how small and alone I am. There are the dots of light below me and the dots of light above me and I have the feeling that I'm floating helplessly between the two planes of light. Above is the void, below is Newton and all the little houses and all the people sleeping peacefully in their own beds. Pop and Charlene are down there, and Mother in her grave back in Houston and that dead boy, my half-brother, I guess he would have been; I don't even know his name. I don't even know what to call my own brother.

I fight off the pity, go looking for something else and what I find almost makes me laugh. Because what strikes me is that I am a lucky man, lucky for lots of reasons to be alive, lucky, you'd have to say, that fate or misfortune or whatever it is sometimes leads us into misery. I'm lucky that once there was a good woman named Kathleen Anderson, nee Flanigan, also known as Katty, who took a used-up man named Henry and led him out of misery, and that together they begat a son, and together they called that son James, also known as Jimbo. I think about that, how it is that I am at least alive and have a name, but it doesn't seem enough, can't be enough, and I go on to think about how good luck and bad luck trade places throughout a life and how each seems to stack up on itself, getting better and better or worse and worse, and how the difference between me and all those people asleep in their houses down the hill is that, for one reason or another, with help or without, they have been able to get through the bad and have somehow made it good and that good luck is really nothing more than peace of mind. That's what I want, peace of mind, to sleep calmly in my own bed, and I hate it that they're in the good and I'm in the bad and that I'm completely lost as to how to get out of it.

Where it comes from, from which part of my mind or my body, I don't know, but I open my mouth and shout into the night, "Listen, people, my name is Jim Anderson and I am a lucky man."

I'm sure that no one hears me, but I stand still listening to the echo, then just listening, feeling my body breathe, and then I walk slowly to the truck, even though I don't know where I'm going. And that's when I find out I was wrong. That's when I hear the voice rolling up the hill from one of the houses down below. He yells, "Who cares?" drawing out the words so that they hang in the night, and then, "So what?" The sound of it bristles my hair and makes me pause, holding the door handle. But then comes the laughter. I laugh quietly, remotely, in little jerks, my eyes tearing up, imagining that other guy down the hill, a man like me maybe but dressed only in a robe and slippers, pacing on the grass of his backyard, smoking a cigarette perhaps, pulling on his hair, trying to figure out whatever it is he needs to figure out when all of a sudden this voice descends on him from the darkness telling him something he really doesn't want to hear. The poor bastard. I laugh and laugh. It feels better knowing I'm not alone. And I mutter at the steering wheel, "You're right, brother. You're absolutely, goddamn right."

The dashboard lights are friendlier now as I drive back to the house. I go in through the kitchen, certain that Pop's worn out and sleeping hard, and then straight to my room. Without care I pack swiftly, stuffing my things into the two suitcases I brought, and as I'm heading out through the living room I stop at the sewing cabinet. In the weak glow from the window I see the thimbles reaching up to me. I kneel until my eyes are level with the thimbles and I look at them like they're a problem I have to solve. I mumble, "Thank you, Mama," but I don't waste time over it. I get a little paper bag out of the kitchen and gently, very gently, drop all the thimbles inside.

The bug light at the porch of Charlene's house is still on when I stop. It shines a yellow cone out into the yard. A dog appears from the darkness, growling raggedly between his teeth, but he passes quickly through the cone. With a pencil from the glove box I write "Charlene" on the bag of thimbles, holding it up in the light that reaches the truck, "from Jimbo." Then I write, "You're a good woman." I put the bag in the mailbox, raise the little red flag and drive away. At the highway I see the sun is about to edge up in the east, a cool orange and pink above South

Dakota, above Mount Rushmore, but I see no faces in the line of clouds that is nothing more than a distant shadow over the horizon. It's like a lesson from sophomore English — so much meaning, so much symbolism: something settled, a new beginning. But it does me no good. I wait, barely breathing, listening to the engine idle quietly, trying to decide which way to go.

A
MINOR
DISTURBANCE

When had it begun — the early rising? She couldn't remember exactly and he wouldn't talk about it, though six weeks was a good guess, just after his father died and he returned home — her home, their home — from the week he took off from work and from her to settle things with his family over in Houston.

Yes, it started when his father died. Poor man.

At first she hadn't noticed any great change at all, except that he was up and about when she woke, with the coffee made and the paper on the table, unopened, the rubber band still taut, holding in the news. No, he wasn't up early to read, and it took him several days to learn the proper proportions of coffee and water and heat and time required to keep out the bitterness. Making the coffee had always been her job and while it was brewing, a brief span of solitude which she enjoyed, she would tend to minor leftover tasks; she picked up the living room or did the dishes from the night before, meaningless things but somehow important to her and necessary.

For ten years she had been the first to rise, the one to open the curtains on the new day and to switch off the outside light, the one to let in the cat and to turn on the heat in wintertime so the house would be warm when he got up. At roughly the same time every morning she would return to the bedroom, seat herself on the bed beside him and gently nudge him out of sleep. Saying nothing in particular, saying whatever came into her head, she would talk to him to get his mind going, and she would rub his arms and his back to stir the circulation, to get his body moving. It was amusing, the garbled things he mumbled while coming out of the spell and the way he would curl up and groan when he realized what was happening. She did this for him, so the annoying alarm would not be the first sound he heard each morning, so it would not crack the dawn peace which they liked to share for a few minutes before showering and dressing and going off to work. She had never needed the alarm — her own inner timepiece served her well — though she routinely set the bedside clock for six o'clock just in case, and then habitually turned it off as soon as her eyes opened. Now he was the one to preempt its mission when he returned each morning to wake her, and the change was unsettling. She remembered something her mother had said years ago: *The first out of bed has the upper hand.* But he was not up early to conquer; she knew this with the same certainty that she knew he was faithful. It was in his eyes.

Then one morning something jostled her out of sleep — it was not him, not the physical him in motion, in the act of rising; it was the absence of him, a certain chill in the bed, an intense quiet, not a breath to be heard, an uncommon calm in the room — and the clock, shining its green numerals above the night stand, blipped at that moment to 4:38. So it's earlier than I suspected, she thought, making her way by instinct through the black tunnel of the hall. She found him sitting in one of the red-wood chairs on the landing, his hair still mussed from the pillow, his robe hanging open over his thick, crossed legs, a slipper dangling from the upheld foot. He moved only his head when he heard her come out and he smiled for her; she saw his face lift slightly in the amber sheen of the porch lamp by the door. The late spring sky was just beginning to pale above the trees in the yard.

"What are you doing out here?" she had asked, stooping beside him, but he only shrugged and said, "Couldn't sleep." Dew glistened on the planks of the landing, the arm of the chair, even his shoulders. "Aren't you cold?" she said and the sound of the word came back to her. She groped for the lapels of her robe and clutched them together at that point on her chest just above her heart. He patted her hand then and meekly touched her hair.

He said, "There's coffee."

"Yes, I smelled it." She took his mug from him, turned it up for a sip from the dregs — cold, bitter, gritty. The damp air whispered in the boughs of the trees. Shivering, she said, "Would you like to talk?" and once again he smiled.

"Not now," he said and then exhaled noisily as if casting out something from his body — something hard yet impalpable.

Back to bed she went for an hour's additional rest against the workday to come, but she found sleep elusive and lay awake as the songbirds started up outside the window. She thought, it's nothing, we all have such nights, a touch of restlessness, that's all. It's nothing.

And the next morning she thought the same, and the

next: it will pass; he is a man of conscience and responsibility and it is to be expected that on occasion he will be troubled and thoughtful. We have much to think about and to concern ourselves with: this is why we have denied ourselves children; this is why we have to pinch and scrape; this is why we work the live-long day, why he goes to that dingy little office every morning to right the wronged sentences of those who think they have something to say; and why I go to my dingy little office to do the mailings and to answer the calls and to encourage them to act as I would act. We have chosen and such a choice is not an easy one; it causes him to reflect, that's all. I'm sure that's all it is. He could have done so many things, he had so many options. It's natural to regret, to wonder how his life might have been.

The man's father has died, for heaven's sake!

And the next morning, when accumulated weariness had upset the inner timepiece and caused her to oversleep, after the willful alarm had rattled so maliciously — he must have forgotten — and she had slapped the little button to hush it: we need to talk, to get it out, to understand it, but he refused, saying it was only a minor disturbance. But what is it? I don't know, he said. He smiled sadly somewhere inside himself and this showed in the movement of his lips: it will pass.

Had it been a biological shift, had there been a corresponding change in the evening, had he begun to bed himself earlier perhaps she would have dismissed it as a mere adjustment in the routines of his life. People do that, certainly; we all do. Yet still it was midnight or sometimes one o'clock before he would put away his work or his reading, and she would feel his weight ease onto the mattress beside her and then hear the long day's final sigh come up from his lungs. Always she reached out to him then as if to make sure that it was flesh and bones lying down beside her and not just the spirit of this good man seeking its nightly repose out of long habit. And always he took her hand then, held it for a moment. This, she thought, was a pact between them that allowed each to put away the turbulent daylight period and to rest, finally, if only for a few hours in his case, though she was uncertain anymore whether he slept at all.

At times she wondered if he made a show of coming to bed only to appease her, to sate her concern, to let her think that he slept at least in those, the earliest, the bleakest hours out of the twenty-four. She did not have the strength or the will to hold off sleep long enough to discover the secret. She knew this: he was gone from the bed when she woke; and the coffee was made and the paper on the table; and the dishes sometimes sat dirty beside the sink now for days at a time. What is it? What's wrong? Nothing, he would say. Nothing. Don't worry.

How odd this was for a man who had always gone about his life with — there was no other word to use but gusto, an exuberance that attracted even small children to him as if they saw the keen, smoldering essence of his living in those dark glittering eyes. It was an exuberance that exhausted him most days. He usually slept like one who relished the peace of it, as if slumber were a daily salvation, a man who, as far as she could tell from what he said, was never troubled by dreams. When they were first married it seemed that those seven, eight, sometimes even nine hours were like a wink to him and that with waking he would start exactly where he had left off the night before.

She was the one who from time to time would lie awake searching the blank ceiling for respite and release; she the one who on infrequent nights roamed the house, her mind unable to let go of some trifle, some slight by a co-worker, some detail of policy over which she disagreed. She was the uncertain one, the restless one — always had been. Such an extravagance, such an indulgence! An indulgence that she dared not allow herself now, during this period, and she lay alone at midnight hoping it would end, thinking that her absence from the lighted parts of the house, her naked presence in the darkened bedroom might coax him out of his disturbance. At times she wanted to call out to him, *Come to me! I am not immune.* But how could she? It would seem an intrusion and selfish. And what if he declined?

Perhaps it was his age. He had turned forty earlier in the year, a difficult number to live with: at least half, perhaps two-thirds of his life, gone, passed away, over with. Mid-life, it was called. She had read about the crises men face and she knew her own confusion, her own thoughts of a neglected past and an uncertain future, and the odd stirrings in her body. It was a time to take measure, to look around, to re-evaluate. His father, whom she had seen only a few times at infrequent family get-togethers, was seventy-two when he went in his sleep just a few weeks ago; his mother had been seventy. Given the probabilities that would mean he had a good thirty years to live. A lot can be done and seen in thirty years. But a close friend had died only last December and he was — what? how old? it was quite disturbing to them both — he was only in his fifties. Let's see, she thought, and I am thirty-eight and his brother — what has he told me? — his brother the businessman, the one who took their father's place and has tried all these years to draw him back into that world. *Come home*, his brother would say, *let's do it together, there's plenty for both of us, no reason for you to deny yourself the way you do. What will you have when you're old?* His brother was forty-four, and twice divorced. And well-off, so comfortable with his two-story house and his new cars, his Junior League wife and all those children making all that noise.

Could it be children? she thought. Is it a child he wants now that he is forty and I am thirty-eight with so little time left? The fertile years peeling away, and that fear of growing old alone and unremembered. What if she were to die — who would he have? She had worried the same worry, looking ahead: what if he were to die? Would there be anyone? They had passed up a chance once when they were first in love, and she had considered a child many times since, though it would have altered every-thing — shattered the well-paced quiet of their lives, strained them financially, hampered them in their causes and careers. Careers! What are careers if we cannot sleep at night together? She would have considered a child, cer-tainly, if he had wanted one. "Just tell me," she muttered in the darkness of the bedroom, pushing away thoughts of how it would bloat her body and deplete her energy in order to imagine a little mouth sucking at her breast. She had seen the affectionate looks he gave the neighborhood children when they played near the yard and the attention he paid his nephews and nieces on their rare visits. He would be a good father, she thought, with his gentle hands and tender heart and his exuberance. What exuberance? He had lost his exuberance, it seemed, at least for her. And where had it gone?

Yes, where had it gone? To another, a younger woman perhaps? A blonde? A redhead, maybe? Someone small and petite and pert? Someone who giggled and fawned? There was that one, the volunteer. But no, she moved away months ago. Who then? He was a handsome man — that cleft and the heavy brow, the easy manner, the way he held himself so erect and ready when listening to someone speak to him at a committee meeting or a party. Sometimes she found herself staring at him at such times and tried to remember just how it was that they had come together, why he had chosen her out of all the women he had known. Twelve years it had been since they first met, first worked together, "raking muck," as he would say. He had the look of a poet in those days, a three- or four-day beard most of the time and crazy long hair. Wavy, graying hair now which he kept trimmed so his face would show. A clear, strong face. That face — he was a handsome man who could have almost anyone. She said, "So tell me then if that's what it is," and her voice fell back upon her in the small dark room. She whispered, "No, don't . . . tell me."

You're being silly, she thought; I would know, I would see it. He didn't have the stealth to hide such things from her. Unless that too, about him, had changed.

Her body moved, legs stretching across the new cool of the sheets on his side of the bed, and something roused within her. Carefully her fingers searched out her breasts, colossal and uncontrollable, the bulging nipples as large as pacifiers, and she thought of the child she had never known, the mistake, taken in a clinic, lost to the practice of their politics and their "personal goals," their youth — youth? Are you young at twenty-seven? And then down her fingers went to the flaccid belly that disgusted her when she examined herself in the mirror — "like a marsupial's pouch," she would jest at those times he watched her in her ablutions. And then down her fingers went to the hips on which she could so easily rest her hands when she stood in position, awaiting the music to start for the exercises that did nothing but make her body ache. And then she imagined herself as a whole: strong, "tall and hefty," as her mother had said in her mean moods, almost as tall as he was and a mere thirty pounds lighter than his masculine bulk — and dark, dark all over. Hair and skin and eyes. Old World Italian eyes that had nothing of her father's fair blue in them. But I like big girls, he would say; and those legs! She wondered about the truth of it, and she hated what was happening to her. The wondering especially.

"Then come to me, if only for my legs," she said, thinking even as she said it: Or is that part of our lives already over?

She heard from somewhere in the house: a door closing? a kitchen cabinet? had he dropped something? And she contained an urge to go see, to help him clean it if it was a mess and then to ask him, Are you all right? Tell me what's wrong. Please tell me.

Once, just a few nights before when she woke alone in the bed at the dreariest hour of all — 3:03, the digits showed — she had gotten up quietly and tiptoed through the house. She paused here, there so as not to startle him, though again she had found him sitting on the landing. At the window by the door she stood, holding open a place in the curtains to look out, and she watched him for a long time. He sat there in the yellow-lighted, dewy haze, smoking a cigarette even though he had quit years ago, and simply looking, out into the trees or beyond, in the way a dog looks about when it has nowhere to go, and then he did something very strange. He leaned forward and held out his cupped hand and he moved his head as if he were speaking to someone, questioning someone, beseeching someone. This went on for a minute or more. She couldn't see his face, but his head wagged up and down and back and forth, and his hand flailed the air for emphasis, and then, when it appeared he had got his answer or had made his point, his arm fell to his side and he slipped into a deep slump in the chair, his shoulders round like an old man's and sort of hangdog, as if the answer had not been the one he wanted. Perhaps he was crying in despair; she couldn't tell and she wanted to go out to him, to sooth him, to comfort him. But she had felt like an eavesdropper or a burglar in her own house, standing there watching him, so she went back to bed and tried to imagine to whom he was speaking.

"Speak to me," she whispered now in an unfocused anger.

She got out of bed. It was 5:44. She had been awake at least an hour. Quickly she made her way through the dark tunnel of the hall, tying the sash of her robe as she went, and at the instant she turned into the living room door, the same door through which she passed every morning, something rose up and stopped her: a bump against her head. She leapt backwards, and a gasp, a silent scream, escaped from deep inside her. It was him.

"My God, you frightened me."

"I'm sorry," he said, standing perfectly still in the doorway. "I was coming to wake you. I have to talk to you."

They stared at each other in a growing silence until the silence drove her to speak, "Yes, good."

He led her out to the landing and more or less put her into her chair and then he said, "I'll be right back." The day was just beginning, with a wan pink light in the east and the first sounds of the birds rustling and chortling in the yard. He returned with two coffee mugs and sat in his chair and then, as if to put her at her ease, as if he were telling a joke at the beginning of a speech, he mentioned the armadillo that visited the yard in the wee hours every morning to root for grubs in the flower beds. "There's no pattern to it, once he's in the yard. Five or ten minutes is all he gives us and then he's gone — next door, I guess. I've seen the marks in the ground during the day but didn't know what they were." He went quiet, reflective. "And there's a deer that comes up out of the woods most mornings — there, just across the road. We'll stare at each other for a few minutes and then she goes away, very quietly and delicately. It's beautiful. Oh, and there's an owl living nearby. I see her two or three times a week, about now in fact." Again he reflected. "You see, I've learned a lot getting up early."

She seized the opening. "What is it you've learned?"

He snorted a quick laugh through his nose, then looked at her and smiled sadly. "I've learned about evil," he said.

This threw her back after the touching way he had spoken of the animals that visited him here in his solitude, and *evil* was not a word she could remember ever hearing him use before. But she said, "In the world, you mean? Evil in the world?"

"No. That I've known of for a long time. It's not the evil you see on the front page, that's not what I mean; it's the evil inside that I've learned about." Suddenly he pointed out above the yard and hissed, "Look! It's the owl." But she was too slow and the bird too swift, and when she turned she saw nothing but the same trees, the same leaves growing restless now under the gathering light. "I missed it," she said and he nodded, smiled as if pleased that he had been able to confirm his earlier report.

The smile fell away quickly and his face reformed itself into the mask of sadness, almost a frown, and, in the quick juxtaposition of the two expressions, she saw how tired he was and she saw that he seemed resigned to his exhaustion, as if it were a permanent state of mind.

"Go on," she said.

Very abruptly he began, "A letter arrived yesterday from

my brother — he's dealing with the estate, you know — and in the letter was a check. . . ." He looked at her as if to see whether she was prepared for him to continue, and she nodded her head to encourage him. "The check is for a lot of money, more money than we could earn together doing what we're doing in ten years. I've known it was coming for some time, but I didn't know it would be so large. We could do anything we want. We could travel. Buy a new house. Anything. To put it simply, we're almost rich."

She couldn't contain her excitement. She said, "I thought your brother had it all in the business."

"No. There was the house. It was in the will."

"Why haven't you told me?"

"Because . . . because we'll have to give it away."

She started to protest, but he stopped her.

"The night before my father passed away I sat in this chair, at this spot — I was just killing time before going in to bed — I sat here and I started thinking about him and how he was and always had been and I remembered things I hadn't thought of in years. Little things, things he had done to me or said to me when I was young, things he would never even remember, things that I hated, and the more I thought about them the more I hated them, and the more I hated them, the more I hated him, the one who had done them, even though I loved him because he was my father. The things I thought about are the sorts of things that go on between all fathers and sons, and, I'd imagine, between all mothers and daughters . . . you know, humiliations and fears and that horrible, horrible longing to please even though you know you can't, could never really please, and that constant feeling that whatever you do it's a disappointment." He paused, thinking, gazing into the trees.

"I remember once," he said and then told her of a summer during college when he had gone home to work at the store with the title of Summer Assistant Manager, and how one day he had been assigned to set up a sale display of lawn mowers. He labored over it all morning, planning it, hanging a banner and signs, lining up the mowers perfectly from the least expensive to the most so the customers could compare. He told her how his father, as he was leaving for lunch with the manager, paused long enough only to say, "No no, they're backwards," and then called over a stock boy, *a stock boy,* to show him how to do it correctly.

"To anyone else in the world he would have said at least, 'Good job, good try,' but not to me, his son. I know it's petty, it's nothing, but I hated it and I hated him. And as I thought about that, and how it's been the same old thing time after time, and how all these years I've had this feeling that I was still waiting really to start my life, even now at the age of forty, and how it would only start when he was gone and I could put him behind me so that whatever I did wouldn't matter anymore because he wouldn't be around, and I wouldn't feel guilty for not doing what he had always wanted me to do — to run that grubby business with my brother — and that night, sitting here in this chair, I wished he would die. Right then. Immediately. . . ."

He went on talking for a long time, confessing secrets as if to a minister with the same sort of energy that pours from an exhausted child explaining *what happened* to make him sin. He even mentioned that at times he had wished she, too, would die so he could start over completely, living exactly the way he had always thought he would live before he had become frightened of the world and decided to marry, but she heard very little of it. She didn't want to hear it and didn't need to hear anymore, now that she knew. Then he cried, and as she held his head against her breasts, muttering, "You poor man," she felt a great release in the regions of her heart, like the release she always felt once a storm arrived. She inhaled a deep breath, exhaled loudly and he must have taken it wrong, as he was unable to see her face, for he mumbled, "Don't cry, it's not you," and she stroked his hair. "I know," she said, and he cried all the more violently. She held him and rocked him gently in the chair to soothe him as he sobbed and then as he whimpered and then as he began to sniffle. It was mostly over now, and she didn't know what to say, so her mind wandered. She thought of the money, but this passed quickly, and she began to think of the many little things, the necessary and important things that she needed to do to prepare them for the day. They would want more coffee and the dishes needed washing and the living room needed picking up. And then she remembered the alarm. It was well past six by now and she imagined the clock's high-pitched electronic pulses assailing the dark serenity of the empty bedroom, and she could almost see the sound it made, like the constant flashing of a buoy's beacon across the waters of a night-hushed lake, and then she could almost feel the rhythmic pulses of the sound coming to her in vibrations through the walls and the floors and the redwood chair, and she knew that would be the first thing she tended to when this ended and they went back inside the house.

Something moved among the trees out over the road and she said, "Oh, look, it's the owl," but he didn't lift his head and when she glanced at her lap she saw that he was sleeping.

THE PIER,
THE PORCH,
THE PEARLY GATES

Millhouse at the wheel. And Helen talking.

"The *Reader's Digest* says you should prepare, buy the things you'll need — appliances, cars, that sort of thing, things that'll last — " She shifted her broad hips on the cracked vinyl seat of the Oldsmobile, the trade-in that for thirteen years had taken them to work and to church at the First Methodist and out to eat on Thursday nights. Her voice dropped, the tone gentle like an undertaker's; she enunciated, " 'So as to ease the transition of retirement and to enrich the last, best years of your life.' "

"Hah!" said Millhouse, working to keep the car between the stripes of his lane. "Rich?" he said. He guided the Oldsmobile, transmission clattering, engine smoking, off the freeway ramp and toward the dealership's used car lot. It chugged, hissed, it died on the access road, blocking traffic at the entrance to the dealership, and a tow truck hauled it away. They were silent with each other for a long time as a salesman showed them different models and took them for a test drive in a Chevette.

"Ain't it great," said the salesman, Johnny, scratching an itch under the penguin on his golf shirt. "Power steering, reinforced suspension, Body by Fisher, just like riding on a cloud." He smiled, "Or in an Oldsmobile."

"It's wonderful," Helen said from the back seat.

"Hah!" said Millhouse, but Johnny, behind his sunglasses, didn't seem to hear. Millhouse drove straight to the dealership, got out, said, "We'll take it."

In the showroom, waiting for the contract, they rested, sipping Cokes, in the front seat of a shiny red Corvette, the price on the sticker half again as much as the price of their first house. He said, "This one, you know, that little car out there, it's going to have to take us to the Pearly Gates."

He knew it would draw her out. He hated her silence; he wanted her to speak. But more, he wanted her to admit it, to acquiesce, to join him in his misery, to say, yes, you're right, after thirty-nine years of struggling, of suffering under the weight of it all, it's over, we're buying an $8,000 coffin. Now, finally, the funeral can begin.

She said, "You're right, Charlie, but at least this one won't break down on the way."

Through his bifocals he saw something of the young Helen in the upper regions of her face — the dead-set brow, the firm straight nose — but something forbidding in the folds of her jowls. He beat the horn with his fist, two quick honks that bellowed through the showroom, and everyone looked over.

He said, "Two points for you."

"If you keep this up, Charlie, we may need a new pickup, too, so we can both get to the Pearly Gates."

He hit the horn again. "Two more points." Everyone was looking, and a suited salesman started toward them. Millhouse waved through the window, grinned, and the salesman stopped, nodded, smiled at the old people, went back to his customers.

Millhouse gripped the wheel of the Corvette until his knuckles went white. He rubbed the bit of arthritis in his hand. He saw disappointment or disgust or humiliation in the glaze of her eyes, the taut mouth, the rigid, almost quivering jaw.

"I'm scared," he said.

She reached out as if to touch him, but held back. She scrounged through her shoulder bag and found his stomach medicine: "Here, take one of these, relax. And please, please Charlie, quit talking about the Pearly Gates."

II

Millhouse at the pier. Millhouse on the porch. It's been two months now and a pattern is developing. Millhouse in his recliner. He has the time now even to dote on himself. Afternoons, gazing into the bathroom mirror, his cup of Folgers cooling on the counter top, he considers the curves and lines of his face. He clips his nose hairs. He strokes his moustache with the tiny purple comb that Helen gave him when he stopped shaving his lip in mute celebration of the end of a career: four decades as a traffic-light specialist for the City of Houston, Harris County, Texas. The moustache came out salt and pepper, not yet the silky white of his hair, so thin and fine to the touch, like the soft brown tufts on the heads of his grandchildren. The lobes hang long, flabby, and the chin has doubled, tripled, but the nose is the same, a slight crook, pointed at the end. An honorable nose.

At the bedroom window, his hands behind his back,

Millhouse thinking: azaleas; I'll plant azaleas for Helen under those four pines in a thick bed of mulch. But it will have to wait: too much to do. Paint, mow, fix the fences, the rotting porch, the septic tank. He wants the place in good shape, easy for Helen to keep up in case . . . in case something happens to him and she is left alone. But where to begin? And the county hasn't had a drop of rain since the week he cleared out his desk. How's a man to work with dehydration always threatening to strangle him?

Millhouse making the bed. The smooth melody of a Harry James tune seeps through the house like a vapor from the long-silent hi-fi he found in a closet of the second bedroom where the girls slept on weekends. He pauses, listens, glances at the pictures on the wall — Sheila, dark, on the left, Gloria, blonde, on the right — and the plaque of APPRECIATION from the City.

Sometimes, when he's feeling up to it, he cooks supper for Helen — chicken pot pies or a frozen pizza, whatever's in the box, hot and on the table when she walks in the door. He enjoys doing it for Helen — Helen, who rolls with life like a cork on waves, who is still working, a new job close to home, not in Houston. She drives in to Huntsville at eight, out from Huntsville at five, in the new Chevette.

Helen is late today. He goes out to the porch to wait, reclining in his lawn chair. On Fridays they used to hurry to get away, drive up to the house, spend the weekend, go back in on Monday. That was then, before he retired and they moved to the old farmhouse for good. He misses the excitement of unlocking the door to a dark kitchen, turning on lights in the close, dark smell, going from room to room to see that nothing had changed.

Here is Helen, easing the Chevy up the driveway to

park it behind the truck. Millhouse brings in the groceries, complaining, "I knew you shouldn't have taken that job."

"I told you I was going to the store after work."

He says, "How am I to remember everything you tell me?" She stops, looks at him closely, kisses his face between two grocery sacks. They put away the perishables and then Millhouse reheats the Spam he fried for supper. "Spam?" she says. "It's all we had." She says, "I told you I was going to the store." They eat in the kitchen and stare into the hole under the counter next to the sink where Millhouse plans to install a dishwasher.

III

It's early morning and Millhouse is at the doctor's office, the third since leaving his job. "I can't find anything," says the doctor, a boy in a blazer. "Tell me again, when do you have these pains?"

"All the time. Whenever I think about my life."

The doctor blushes and fidgets, says not to worry, it will pass, and he gives Millhouse a prescription for sleeping pills. In the truck Millhouse wads up the prescription and throws it out the window. He doesn't know why he keeps going to doctors except that it's paid for, mostly, by insurance and that Helen wants to be sure. "At your age, better safe than sorry," she says, but she misunderstands him when he talks of pain.

He stops at the pier to look at the lake, just look. A thin fog still curls over the water, obscuring the far shore. The glassy surface of the lake appears solid, impenetrable, the cove deep and lifeless, somehow frightening. He stares trancelike at the water until a fish breaks through, sending out its concentric circles like a message to the shore. The quiet closes in on him, so he gets in the truck and goes home.

At noon the postman's jeep appears on the road. Millhouse stalks down the driveway, looks inside the mailbox and takes out the small brown envelope. Handling it, turning it over, he reads the fine print on the back and waits several minutes before ripping open the seal.

～

The afternoon burns amber outside the windows of the bank in Huntsville. Millhouse fills out a deposit slip and gives it to the teller, young and pleasant, a black woman with a strand of pearls around her neck. "It's my first one," says Millhouse. "My first check from the government. Like Welfare." He grins.

"Ah," she says, letting it linger in the air, moving her hands over the machine. "Congratulations. You should frame it."

"Naw," he says and sort of laughs.

"Enjoy," says the teller, handing Millhouse his receipt.

Outside he gets into the pickup, sweltering from the sun, and drives down Bowie Street. He passes the Walgreen's where he gets a Senior Citizen's Discount and then stops at Hank's Lumber and Hardware. Almost everyone at Hank's knows Millhouse by now and he waves to a couple of men as he makes his way past the heavy green nail buckets and the row of lawn mowers to Helen's office. She's doing the inventory ledgers. He can see her through the glass in the door, the big books open on her desk, the finger working the adding machine one key at a time.

"What are you doing here?" She's cheerful, glad to see him.

"The bank. It came."

"I knew something good was going to happen today. Was it what you thought it would be?"

"Two dollars more."

"Well, see. I told you it wouldn't be so bad." She gets a satisfied look on her face. "You can buy yourself a lime freeze for the ride home. I saw that Dairy Queen's got a special on."

They talk for a while and she tells him that Gloria called to say she and Roger will bring Josh up on Saturday. Josh is their eldest grandchild and he spends a week with them every year during their vacation. But Helen won't get vacation this year.

"She said all he's been able to talk about since school let out is Papaw, Papaw. He wants you to teach him how to fish."

"For a whole week?"

Her face oozes mirth. It's that grin that used to infuriate him with its shrewd, teasing squinch around the eyes. Now he knows it's just Helen and accepts it as he accepts the smelly Ben-Gay rubs she gives him when he's been working on the land.

"I'm afraid it's two weeks," she says as if she's about to laugh. "Gloria promised him."

Millhouse remembers the noise, the questions, the broken keepsakes, the general trauma Josh inflicts on their lives when he comes to visit: "He'll drive you crazy."

"It's not me . . . " she says. "Oh, Charlie, you'll enjoy it. He sure loves his Papaw." She glances around quickly and then kisses him on the cheek. "Now go. I've got work."

On his way out he hears one of the salesmen call to him from across the showroom: "Have you caught the big one yet?" He's holding his hands in front of him as if approximating the length of a yardstick.

Millhouse isn't sure he understood and, with an exaggerated tilt of his head, cups his ear to get him to repeat it.

"The big bass," the man hollers between hands now shaped around his mouth like a megaphone.

"Ah," Millhouse calls back. "I'm trying."

The man yells, but not quite loud enough: "I wish I . . . leisure . . . take it easy. . . ."

Millhouse nods and waves and walks out the door to the parking lot. "Leisure." He spits the word at the truck and then gets inside. He drives up Lamar to Main Street and cruises the business district, watching the small-town, county-seat activity. He sees a HELP WANTED sign in the window of the Western Auto. Craning over the steering wheel, he tries to look into the store but the glare of the sun is too great and all he can see is the reflection of the truck sliding by in ripples across the glass.

～

Millhouse at the Dairy Queen. Millhouse in the truck, sucking on a lime freeze through a straw. The drive from town to home is 18.2 miles. There are clusters of houses along the way, some farms and ranches, railroad tracks and acres of trees. He turns onto the dirt road that leads to the house and waves to Grady atop his tractor, Grady who retired last year and bought the Jenson place with cash savings at the same time he and Helen paid off their mortgage. Grady is mowing what's left from the drought of the coastal Bermuda he planted on his eight acres.

Millhouse and Grady often argue about grass. Millhouse knows for a fact that Bahia is sturdier than Bermuda, but Grady won't listen. He was an engineer and thinks he knows everything. One thing about him, though: he has self-respect; he keeps his place up. He's painted it, repaired the pump house, cleared the land where it needed it. People talk about how pretty it is, how Grady "really saved that spread" after old Jenson let it "dilapidate."

The tractor stops out in the field and Grady crawls

down, starts walking toward the road. Millhouse presses the accelerator and then watches in the mirror as big flags of dust billow up behind the tailgate.

At home he goes to the storage shed off the garage. It's cool and damp and crowded with lumber he's purchased to build or repair things around the house, and boxes. One of the boxes, a large one, came from Sears and contains the dishwasher they bought before he retired. Josh's old crib, dismantled, leans against the wall in the corner near a pyramid of new paint cans.

He finds his fishing gear. The eyes on the poles are green with corrosion, one of the reels stiff with age. The tackle box is practically empty — some twisted line and a few gnarled hooks, an old hunting knife wrapped in foil. He unwraps the knife and runs his thumb along its rusty blade. The blade pricks his finger and a dollop of blood bubbles up. He licks it away, salty and earthy on his tongue. He says, "I hate fishing." It echoes in the shed and startles him, as if someone may have heard. He lays the poles and the tackle box behind the stacks of lumber where no one can see them, then goes outside to the yard. The horse is grazing in the pasture just down the fence line. Millhouse stops at the fence, calls, "Hey, Knuckles," but she doesn't look up.

~

Millhouse snacking on peanut butter and crackers over the sink, squinting to read the thermometer outside the kitchen window — 96. He makes his afternoon pot of coffee and sits for a while at the table. Millhouse on the phone to Helen.

"You're going to have to call Gloria back," he says. "Tell them I'm not feeling well or something."

"But Charlie, he'll be so disappointed."

"I tell you I don't want to. I don't know how to fish, it's been years. And what if he were to drown or something?"

"Drown?" Her voice is high, stretched with sarcasm. "Charlie, you're being silly. You used to fish all the time."

"I don't want to argue, Helen. And this is long distance."

"Charlie — " she begins, but he hangs up. He stares at the phone and then picks up the receiver. He puts it down again when he hears a car pass on the road, and goes out to pick up the newspaper. Back inside he pops the rubber band, pops it, pops it until it breaks, then he sits at the table, scanning the front page. He reads a story about delays in a street-paving project in Houston, and in the story is the name of a city spokesman he's never heard or seen before. That was Hardy's job: City Spokesman. Where is he? What's happened? Already it's changed. He moves on to other news, sees hundreds of words, some large, some small, but doesn't read them. The words are about Houston and the world and have nothing to say to him now.

He rolls up the paper as if the rubber band were still around it and then he throws it with all his might across the room. Pages come loose and fly everywhere, but the core of the newspaper smacks a lamp and sends it crashing to the floor. He looks at the mess and mutters, "This is how I knew it would be."

IV

Millhouse, still in his robe, watching a game show on TV. He hears a horn blowing outside. It's Grady in his truck.

"Man, aren't you up yet?" Grady calls through his window.

"I'm not feeling too well."

"No time for that. Come on. I need some help."

"I can't today."

"It's just some logs."

"Can't today."

"See you in a few minutes."

Grady's truck rolls backwards down the driveway.

He yells, "I can't," but knows Grady can't hear him. "You old loon." Millhouse in the bedroom, putting on jeans, cursing Grady, putting on a shirt and his boots, his cap. He leaves.

Grady, with a foot on a log, is waiting for Millhouse as he walks slowly across Grady's pasture toward the felled tree.

"This'll get us through the winter," Grady says, nodding to the litter of timber before him, and Millhouse grunts a reply. Together they lift logs into the bed of Grady's truck.

"Where you been the past few days?" says Grady, wiping sweat from his big-nosed face with a bandana.

"Busy."

"Fixing the fence?"

"Nope."

They heave logs until they've made a load. Then they get inside. Grady directs the truck toward the woodpile. They bounce over the rough spots in the pasture and Grady complains about the pinched disc in his back. They drop off the logs and return for another load. Millhouse can feel Grady eyeing him.

He says, "Something on your mind?"

"Yeah, as a matter of fact," says Grady. "As a matter of fact I do have something to say. I think you're sitting on your can over there, kind of just waiting for something to happen, and I think that's stupid. There's work to do."

Millhouse feels a terrific lurch in his chest. He turns on Grady. He says, "Stop the truck."

Grady looks incredulous under his heavy gray eyebrows.

"I said, stop the truck."

Millhouse gets out and strides across the pasture toward his own pickup. Grady yells, "See you later, eh Charlie? Eh?" Then louder: "Eh?" Millhouse doesn't look back.

⁓

At home he lays down on the bed to think. He remembers the HELP WANTED sign at the Western Auto in Huntsville, wonders what sort of job it would be. But his mind turns quickly. He imagines the pistol in the bottom drawer of the dresser. It's wrapped in a towel under his sweaters. There's a box of bullets in the drawer too. Now he sees himself in the shed, sitting on a stack of lumber, holding the barrel of the pistol to his temple as he has seen them do in the movies. Or, no, the mouth; he'd do it through the mouth. His face is serious-looking and deathly white.

The phone rings and Millhouse gets up to answer it.

Gloria says, "Hi, Daddy."

"Hello, Sugar," he says, wishing he'd stayed in bed, knowing he'll have to lie. They chat for a few minutes and Millhouse tells her that he's feeling better, but still not well enough to look after Josh for two weeks. And suddenly Gloria is crying.

"Oh, Daddy, we're in trouble."

She says Roger has been talking about moving out. He's not sure he loves her. She was hoping they could have a couple of weeks to themselves. Would he please take Josh?

He thinks he should console her, but this has happened before and he doesn't want to know any more about it. He should say simply, no, I can't this time. Instead, he says, "All right, all right, bring him up. But there won't be any fishing."

Her voice is weak but tinged with hope. "Thank you, Daddy."

⁓

Millhouse at the pier. He sits down, takes off shoes and socks, lets his feet dangle in the water. The ducks that make the cove their home squawk about the intrusion, but glide by in twos and threes, watching him, he thinks, in case he has brought food. He hears someone drive up behind him on the narrow road through the woods. It's Grady, with an ice chest.

"Thought you might be here," Grady says and sits on the ice chest at the edge of the pier. "I've got some beer, you want one? Nothing like a cool one after a hard day's work."

Millhouse seldom drinks, but this time he accepts. He sits silently as they sip their first beers and Grady comments on the drought — sixty-five days without a drop — and how he's going to lose the rest of his grass unless they get some rain. Millhouse doesn't say what he wants to say about grasses, but soon, his tongue loosened by liquor, he ventures a few words and they start to talk. They talk as novices about the qualities of different brands of beer and of drinking bouts they had as young men, laughing occasionally, lapsing into silence. They talk about hunting trips they may or may not take. They drink and talk about nothing in particular until the sun is low across the lake and there are eleven empty cans floating in the chilly water at the bottom of the ice chest. "You want the last one?" Grady says.

"Naw, you go ahead," says Millhouse. He stands up, woozy, and holds onto the top of a pile for support. Everything appears blurry. When he gets his balance he notices that the water is calm, a cool brown, somehow inviting in the heat. He can see the reflection of the trees around the lake, the glare of the sun.

Grady says, "Hey, old man, you okay?"

Millhouse doesn't answer, but he takes off his glasses

and sets them on top of the pile. Then he leaps off the
pier, pulling his knees up, and smacks the water hard with
his butt. Under the surface he feels an instant of panic; it
has been a long time since he was in water above his
knees. After a moment, though, he relaxes, opening his
eyes, holding his breath, and spreads his legs and arms. It
comes back to him; he swims easily and, he thinks, gracefully. And he has been wrong about the underwater life of
the lake, the cove. There are plants dancing on the cold
bottom and rocks and a tennis shoe and a slimy-looking
length of ski rope. Everything is peaceful but has an eerie,
unreal quality in the cloudy water, which isn't as deep as
he has imagined.

"A cannonball," Grady cries when Millhouse comes up.

He sees that Grady has an approving look on his face,
as if he wishes he had been the one to do it. Then Grady
jumps in too, boots and all, holding the beer can above his
head. They stand there, the water line at their chests, silver hair matted to their heads, passing the can back and
forth, grinning at each other as if to say, What the hell are
we doing?

V

Millhouse wakes in the night with a cramp in his thigh.
And he wakes in the morning feeling groggy, lumpy. A
hangover. Helen brings him coffee in bed and puts two
aspirin on the night stand. She is dressed for work and in a
hurry. From the foot of the bed she smiles at him as she
would smile at a child who has done something cute. "Are
you in pain?" she asks.

"Extreme," he says, but she doesn't understand.

Heavy-headed, he slips back to sleep without taking the
pills and wakes up at one, his leg still stiff from the cramp.
He watches television, queasy in his stomach, until

late-afternoon when he gets hungry. At the sink in the kitchen he eats ham and cheese on leftover toast. The faucet is dripping; Helen has asked him to fix it. He turns the handle hard until it stops. Through the window he sees Knuckles dragging herself across the drought-yellowed pasture toward the fence. It's feeding time. Sweat stings his eyes as he goes to the shed, digs up a bucket of oats, walks to the fence and pours it over into the trough. He tosses the bucket into the shed and starts toward the house, but then, at the woodpile, he notices something moving among the logs. It's a snake, a big copperhead, now sunning itself on a stump.

Millhouse hurries into the house and down the hall to the bedroom. He takes the pistol and the box of bullets out of the drawer. He loads the gun quickly, not wanting the snake to get away, to hide somewhere so that Josh may stumble upon him. But outside he finds that the snake hasn't moved. Millhouse, who has fired the pistol only a few times, aims it at the snake's head, an easy target, though his hand shakes a little.

He pulls the trigger and the gun's explosion echoes through the surrounding woods. But he missed — "I missed!" — and still the snake simply lies there, at peace in the spring sun, completely unaware that it is about to be cast into everlasting darkness, that it will breed no more offspring, that it will stalk no more prey, that it will never again wake from the sweet silence of hibernation. How lucky, thinks Millhouse, and he lowers the gun, looks at it. The pistol's sharp edges become hazy. He blinks, trying to focus, and a close thunder pounds through his head.

He drags himself to the shed and sits down heavily on the stacks of lumber. The pistol and his arms hang limp between his legs. It's cool in the shed and this reminds him of the pump house on Grady's place where they found old man Jenson. Neighbors said that he died of a heart attack while repairing the pump, but Millhouse has often wondered. There is a nasty stain on the wall in there and he thinks it is blood. He now feels his own blood pulsing through his temples, drumming his brain, prickling his hair. He looks at the gun and then points the barrel at the sideburn on the right side of his head, just to see how it feels, to learn if it feels the way he has imagined. But he was wrong: the barrel seems to press against his brain — it is actually touching him — and the blood pulses.

This is not how he saw it: opening wide, he slips the barrel between his lips. He can taste oil and the metal is warm on his tongue; the sight pricks the roof of his mouth. He imagines what he would look like to someone watching him just now: stupid, silly. What if it were Josh? *Hey, Papaw, what are you doing?*

Uncomfortable, he shifts his body, and then something happens. The plank on which he is sitting slips from under him, slides to the next lower stack and sends him bouncing painfully to the ground. He lets out a gasp when the gun sight rakes across the tender skin in his mouth and he tastes blood mingling with the oil. "Stupid, stupid," he mutters and lifts the pistol as if to throw it. He sits still, his pant legs in the dust, his back against the lumber.

From here he can see FRAGILE stenciled on the box containing the dishwasher and the labels on the paint cans. On each of the labels is a man's face and each identical face has a challenging smile, the same smile that enlivens Grady's eyes when he acts like he knows everything. He can see Grady looking down at him, shaking his head the way his neighbors shook their heads over the death of old Jenson. One thing about Jenson: he had no self-respect. He would go for weeks in the same overalls and shirt; his place always looked abandoned. His wife, left destitute with a dilapidated house and barn, fields overrun by clover, had to sell the farm — that Grady, he got it for a prayer, fixed it up, working eight hours a day, wearing his jeans and boots as if they were a uniform, as if he were a baker or a postman or a ranch hand: "This is what I do now," he said once. "It's my job." — and Mrs. Jenson had to move to the nursing home in Huntsville.

She, too, is of the dead now, at peace beside her husband, one of those for whom death was a reward. Something moves deep in his intestines and he tries to swallow. He imagines Helen, humiliated, standing on the crumbling porch, barking like an auctioneer to a crowd of strangers whose legs are hidden in the waist-high grass. They'd steal her blind, he thinks, and images come to him of all the things he needs to do.

He's been wanting to dig a pond for the livestock down where the pasture becomes a bog when it rains. Grady would help; they'd rent a backhoe. They'd work only in the cool of the mornings, digging and smoothing out the dirt, banking it up to hold the water. And after lunch they would go to the cove and sit on the pier, sip beers and talk about hunting trips in the fall. And maybe they'll do it too. Run up to Trinity for some ducks, or over to Uvalde for some doves. The truck's in good shape. And there'll be Christmas, the whole family out from the city, and a fire in the fireplace and holly wreaths on the doors and the sounds of children in the house. And in the spring he'll plant hay with Grady who says they can go in together, sell the excess and make some cash. And he'll plant peach trees in the yard. Yes, he'll have an orchard and put in azaleas for Helen.

Helen. Next summer, July 2 to be exact, she'll retire. That's all she talks about. *Everything will be fine when I'm home for good.* She doesn't know any better. And she wants a vacation. All those years they worked downtown, making a good living together, raising two good children, they never took a vacation outside of Texas. She wants Colorado. Sure, he'd like to see the Rockies. He's read about it. Great Gorge and Cripple Creek and Garden of the Gods. Maybe they'll go up to Yellowstone too, see Old Faithful and the grizzly bears. He ought to see Yellowstone before he knocks on the Pearly Gates.

Millhouse hears something and looks up. Helen is standing in the doorway, her hair frazzled from a day's work, her purse hanging from her hand. She says something about a snake in the woodpile, but cuts it off. She says, "Charlie," as if it's two words. "What are you doing?"

He pulls himself to his knees, the gun still in his hand, and moves awkwardly toward her. "Helen," he says. His voice is high and rough, almost a whimper. He wraps his arms around her thighs, rolls his head back to look up at her face. He wants to explain but when he opens his mouth all that comes out is "Helen." And then: "Let's take a ride, you and me. Come on, let's go to the lake."

She touches his head. She kneels. They face each other, miniatures of themselves on the dusty floor of the shed, she with her purse, he with his pistol. Helen glances at the gun, says, "Oh, Charlie," and he hugs her tightly, achingly to his body.

VI

On Saturday Millhouse gets up early. By the time Helen wakes he has planned his repairs for the faucet and has started on the lawn, knowing the growl of the mower would bring her out. He catches a butterfly and gives it to her. She frees it and then smiles shyly, still frightened, he thinks, of what might be on his mind and in his heart. So he winks at her boldly.

All morning, while Helen washes clothes and cooks a roast, Millhouse watches the sky as dark promising clouds move in from the west, obliterating the sun. Sprinkles come and go, hissing as they strike the hot engine and, after he puts away the mower, pattering among the leaves of the trees. But it never really rains — maybe tonight, or tomorrow — and when Gloria and Roger and Josh arrive, Millhouse is waiting for them on the porch. The car stops, a door opens and here comes Josh, his blond hair flying, running toward Millhouse. He throws himself into his grandfather's arms, screaming, "Papaw, Papaw," and his little hand smacks Millhouse on the jaw, reviving for just a moment the pain of the wound in the old man's mouth.

Millhouse at the pier, sitting beside Josh, who flicks the pole to make the orange cork bob on the brown water.

FURNITURE

What I know I can tell in one word — *furniture*. That's my line; I sell furniture on commission at a small retail outlet in an old clapboard neighborhood of Houston. Our customers are poor, most of them, blue-collar types who've more than likely averaged a job a year and been repossessed once or twice. Some are convicts — we require cash of them — but most, I'd have to say, are what my grandmother called the salt of the earth, people trying to get by on the little bit that God Almighty and the economics of this Great Land of Ours have seen fit to give them.

I've known all kinds. They come in looking for security, I call it, the security that the buying of furniture can provide. Feathering the nest, my wife Sherry likes to say. They're settling in, fixing a home. And when we can make a deal, sign the papers, they go out happy, laughing, talking like you're their best friend or their big brother. It's

a good feeling to send people on their way after giving
them what they want.

It's not always that way, though, and I know it far too
well. Thirty-one years I've beat the linoleum at Green's
Discount, worn out so many pairs of black wing tips that I
long ago lost count, and I've seen sorrow, smelled the hurt,
heard the pain in voices. It still amazes me what people
show of themselves to a perfect stranger. I guess the nest-
ing instinct is strong in people, and the wanting. Wanting,
I've observed, and loss, too, these are what lead to sorrow
and the hurt of living. When I think of this — well, it's a
clear memory that comes to me: of the short skinny man
with a violent temper and of his tall fat wife whose eyes
teared up so easily.

And then there's Sherry, and Darlene, and Gene Junior,
of course, dead in the war.

⁓

"We're just looking," said the husband when they came
in the first time. It was a Friday; Friday's the day the big
truck comes and I recall the floor being crowded with
hampers of new merchandise. I had met them at the glass
doors up front. When a couple comes in, you hustle to get
there ahead of the other salesmen.

"Look all you want," I said and fell into pace behind
them. "My name's Gene. Gene Harris. Give a yell if I can
be of help."

She gave me a nod, but he didn't. They sauntered up
the center aisle past the appliances — washers and stoves
gleaming white and copper and harvest gold — they
paused for a moment, glancing at each other, and then she
pulled him into Furniture.

"We've got a big sale on," I said.

"That so," said the man coldly, but the woman smiled

for me, showing off a big gold tooth sparkling right up front.

"Care for some coffee?" I asked. If you can get them holding onto something then nine times out of ten they're yours for good.

"No, thanks," he said, trying to pretend I wasn't there. The woman smiled again though. She was young, very early twenties at best, with the kind of skin that brings to mind rich dairy products such as buttermilk. I don't mean to be cruel, but this woman was large, more than over-weight. Shoulders like huge Christmas hams, forearms like Popeye the Sailor's and a pair of breasts so large she could have fed the whole state of Texas.

"How's about you, ma'am. A cup?"

"Well . . . " she began but quickly hushed herself and the husband gave me a glare the likes of which I hadn't seen in a while. So I excused myself and slinked off to the sales counter, sort of a corral at the center of the store, where I waited, watching those people. They'd linger here and there, inspect a chair or a coffee table, move together, discuss it. It was apparent they were country types. He was lean, wiry like a fighting cock, and at least ten years older than his wife I'd say by the way he held himself and the fact that his face had obvi-ously begun the downward slide of real maturity. He was so short it seemed his wife spoke into a hole in his blue work cap.

Darlene's chair scraped against the floor and I felt her next to me across the counter. Darlene was the head office girl back then, a pretty, puffed-up, made-up redhead with more pearly teeth than a mattress has springs. She took payments, kept the books, actually ran the store in all practical matters.

"Looks like you got one there," she said, eyeing the people as they meandered through the French provincial and into the Early American. We had a bright new Early American suite from Bassett on the floor and I was hoping they'd stop and take a seat, bounce on the cushions, get a feel. We both watched.

"They're nibbling, sure enough," Darlene said

"I don't know," I said. "I think they're lookers."

"Naw, she's wanting. I can tell."

"How's that?"

"When you're that young, you're always wanting."

Darlene was smiling at me in her appealing way. We were having a time together just then, and once or twice a week I'd follow her home at the end of the day, and we went out on a regular basis for lunch or a cup down at the drug store.

"What's it like — being that young, I mean. You remember?"

She gave me a look teasing with insult and slapped my arm.

"You know I didn't mean anything," I said.

"Take it easy." Her voice was husky — too many Chesterfields.

"Well, then tell me," I said. "What's it like?"

"Good, mostly. But not always. You're always wanting. Look at her. She wants it so bad it's dripping from her eyes."

I looked but I couldn't see it.

"Just what is it she wants?"

"Besides furniture, you mean?"

"Yeah, that's what I mean, Miss Psychology Professor."

"Now that I don't know," she said, twisting up her eyebrows. "Love, or a child maybe . . . who knows what anybody really wants."

We were quiet for a while, both of us thinking, then I

said, sort of whimsical, "Would you want to be that young again?"

"Sure, I'd want to be young again."

"Even with all the longing and the wanting?"

"Even with that, sure. Wouldn't you?"

"Even with the acne and everything stirred up all the time?"

"Sure," she said. "What's got into you?"

I didn't answer. I said, "And what would you do different?"

She grinned, showing lots of teeth, showing off her heart.

"I'd marry you," she said. Then she slapped my arm again and laughed. She could be a hard woman, had to be hard to get by in a life that had left behind two husbands and a boyfriend that knuckled the fire out of her one night and later went to jail for it. But all of that was long ago and there were times when I really felt for Darlene. There were times when I loved Darlene.

"How's about coffee later?" I said and her red-painted lips crested into a smile.

∼

Given what happened, I couldn't get my new "customers" off my mind. So at supper that night I told Sherry, my wife, all about those people, the McCarthy's. I told her how I had sashayed back over toward them, calling out above the lamp shades, "That couch fits you just like a new hat," and how they both stood up then, acting flustered like they'd been caught shoplifting, acting like for some reason they weren't good enough to sit on our furniture.

"Ready to take it home?" I said.

The man snapped, "No no," but his wife, running her

eyes over the pretty fabric, cooed to herself and to me, "Sure is nice, comfortable too," and he gave her a hard look, a cold look. I told Sherry how the woman cowered then, if you can say that a woman of that size could ever really cower, and how the husband more or less strutted back and forth with his hands in his pockets like he was thinking too much about something, and how he suddenly stopped, giving me the same hard cold look he'd given his wife a moment before. I mentioned how he'd done an about-face then as sharply as a soldier in formation and how he marched toward the front, weaving through the furniture and the appliances until he placed his hand on the door. That's when he glanced back, expectant, as if his wife were a dog who came on that kind of simple, stern command.

"He likes to take his time about such things," the wife said. And I'd swear her lashes were batting back tears.

"Yes, ma'am," I said.

"And we've had a death in the family, you see."

"Yes, ma'am," I said, trying to be gentle.

"Well," said the wife, "I better go," and she started off after her husband. "We may be back," she called to me. Smiling, she showed me that gold tooth for just an instant.

I told Sherry what the woman had said and how the husband had given the wife a heap of nasty grief when she got to him at the door, and how he grabbed her arm as if she were a naughty child and spoke right into her chin while he pulled her by the elbow down to his level. I explained how he yanked her out the door and how she stumbled and how her hand came up to her mouth, the backs of her knuckles just barely touching those heavy soft lips of hers as if she were gasping, as if she'd just witnessed some horrible accident in the street.

Darlene and I and everyone else watched then as the husband dragged his wife by the arm out to a pickup waiting in the lot. And we watched even as the truck pulled away, coughing out black smoke so thick that anybody could see the man needed a ring job.

I said, "Are you sure you'd want to be that young again?"

Darlene just grinned and lit up a Chesterfield.

I didn't tell Sherry about my conversation with Darlene — I never mentioned one to the other — but I did tell her about the strange feeling I'd had the rest of the day after those people left the store and how I hoped they wouldn't come back.

"They're probably an unhealthy credit risk anyway," she said, mopping up the last of her gravy with her home-made bread.

I got whimsical again. "Imagine being that young."

She swallowed and said, "No way."

"How's that?"

"Not for me," she said, leaning back and reaching for a Winston. "I'm quite comfortable with the ripe old age of forty-five. All's I want now is for Gene Junior to get himself home from the war, find himself a pretty wife and fill up the house with grandkids. It's a powerful longing in me. I can't wait to help 'em do up their house."

I said, "You wouldn't want to be a sweet twenty-one again?"

She looked at me. "You can have it."

"Even with all the energy you had?"

"Even with all the energy."

"Even with all the good times?"

"What good times?"

This caught me short, but we smiled at each other.

I said, "We had some good times, didn't we?"

"If we did," she said, "I sure can't remember any of them."

"And just what do you remember, Ms. Hardass Housewife?"

Her sage look came on then, mouth lifting slightly at the edges, eyes going to wrinkled slits. She exhaled and a lungful of bluish smoke drifted over the table in my direc-tion. She said, "I remember wondering for three hellish years if you'd ever come back from your war. And then when you did all's I remember is a lot of screaming and slapping and the slamming of doors. And I remember going home to Mother and you coming in drunk and mean late at night and acting like you wanted to beat hell out of me and Mama having to put herself between us to keep you from doing it." Her eyebrows rose, dropped. "That's what I remember."

"But it changed, of course," I said. "Didn't it change?"

She shrugged. Then she got up and started clearing the table, adjusting the Winston with her teeth so that it poked out of her unpainted lips at an angle. She moved around our old Dixieland dinette with ease, a kind of grace that had developed in her only within the past few years. I watched her move, heard the faint rustle of materi-al across her hips, a mother's hips.

I said, "It wasn't all bad, was it, Sherry?"

She grinned through the smoke, glanced at me, took a long drag on the Winston. "We had our moments, I guess," she said.

Sherry went into the kitchen, her arms heavy with dishes, and then her voice — low, lazy, an Atlanta girl's voice — came back through the swinging door: "You want coffee with your pie?"

~

It was about mid-morning that Saturday when Darlene called my name over the loudspeaker. A customer was waiting for me at the corral. I saw the big woman as soon as I turned the corner into the center aisle. She was standing at the counter, solemn as marble, gazing at the TVs flashing against the far wall. Then I saw her husband, strutting among the ranges and washers up front.

"When d'you want it delivered?" I said, coming up behind her. She showed me that tooth in a startled smile, but then her eyes found something on the floor that held them there and wouldn't let them rise. Embarrassment is what it was, and I thought about how brave she had to be to come back into a place where just the day before a dozen people had seen her humiliated.

"Mr. Harris," she began but I interrupted: "Call me Gene."

"Gene, then," she said. "My husband wants to talk to you."

Together we walked toward the front of the store and as the heels of my wing tips smacked the linoleum I could feel something deep within me banking up against my guts. I didn't appreciate the way he'd sent his nice wife like a servant to fetch me and I didn't like the thrown-back angle of his shoulders which revealed an attitude of the sort that told the world it owed him something he shouldn't have to pay for like the rest of us. I'm no Puritan and I know that each of us has to make his way in life as best he can, but the thought of deadbeats and bullies really boils my blood, so that by the time we reached her husband I was angry, and that's no way for a salesman to be.

"Lookie here," he said, scratching at the floor with a boot. His jaw was gray with stubble. "We need furniture. She wants some."

"Yessir," I said. "I figured as much."

"And we got to have it on credit." He made a sound through his nose like a horse, like he was disgusted.

So she threw in, "We got fifty we can give you right away, Mr. Harris, and the truck's parked just out front."

"Hush, Julie Ann," he said. "Let me handle this." She cowered again and I could feel the heat of anger moving across my belly and up my chest. He continued, "Like she said, we got fifty to give you today and we'll pay out the rest ten dollars a month. I just need some help loading it on the truck."

I laughed then, and felt good for it. I told him that wasn't how it worked, that he'd have to fill out a credit application and that the application would have to be checked for accuracy and that we'd need to know some of their history and that the manager would decide how much down payment we'd require and what the payments would be. I mentioned interest rates and the credit bureau and how we had to protect ourselves against risk as best we could, but that I was sure we could make a deal satisfactory to both parties. By the time I was finished he was so red in the face I thought he was going to start bleeding at the nose. He gave his wife that hard cold look again and then he turned on me.

He said, "Just what in hell is this, mister?"

"Mr. McCarthy, that's the way it's done."

He looked at his wife again, a mean glare, and I hated the look. "Had to push it, didn't you, Julie Ann. You really want them to know all about me? Do you?"

She tried to speak, but he raised his hand as if to smack her so that I had to say, "Here, now!" and step between them.

"He don't hit me, Mr. Harris, he just gets frazzled sometimes since the boy passed on."

"Yes, ma'am, I can see that."

"Shut up," he said to her. "L. Junior'd still be alive today if you had a lick of sense in your head." And that's when she started crying, a low rumbling noise rolling up out of her deepest gut, whimpering through her nose. He cursed then and squeezed between us, literally shoved her out of the way, and at the center aisle he looked back. "Come on, gal," he said, but he didn't wait. He was outside before she could get her body moving. The wife followed him out with her eyes, and here's the strange thing: there was a look of love in her face, of love and regret and harsh wisdom, a look that I didn't understand then.

"Ain't there no way, Mr. Harris?" the wife whimpered.

"Not without proper credit, ma'am."

She nodded her head and dug in the pocket of her house dress for a hanky or a tissue but came up empty — ran a sleeve across her nose. Like a lake after a squall, she calmed quickly then.

"He's not always like this, Mr. Harris," she said. "Only since L. Junior died and he started blaming me for it. And I'm just sure as I can be that if we could fix up our place, make it into a real home, you know, everything would get back to normal."

"Yes, ma'am, I know what you mean."

"That was a fine time, Mr. Harris, a fine time. Until he — . He weren't even two year old when he fell in the tank. I was hanging up wash, you see, and not paying attention." She wanted to say this to someone, someone like me, I think, who helped people settle in. "I'm sorry you had to see this," she went on. "He's a good man mostly who's had trouble in his life, that's all."

"Yes, ma'am," I said, thinking I was ready for a coffee break with Darlene. I felt like I had failed in a duty. I needed a cup, and I knew Darlene would want to hear everything these people had said. I thought about the forgiving smells of coffee and toast that would fill our noses when we walked into Randolph's Drugstore and took our seats at the end of the counter.

"You're a real nice man, Mr. Harris," she said, showing me that gold tooth. "And a good salesman too."

"Not good enough, I guess."

"Maybe we'll be back," she said and pushed open the door.

~

I remember that Saturday every year about now, as it just happened to be the day that Sherry received a telegram informing us that Gene Junior was Missing In Action in Vietnam. It was odd, I know, an eerie and unlikely coincidence, but the memory grabs whatever advantage comes along, lest we forget. And there was this too: for several days I'd been having this feeling that kept me awake at night and distracted during the day; it had kept my bowels disturbed and my head kind of light; and I thought it had something to do with Darlene, that I was wanting to start over somehow with her and her appealing ways. Perhaps I just wanted to be young again, not that it's possible, but we all have imaginations and memories and isn't the idea of youth just as real as youth itself? Well now I know: this was only part of it, the weariness, the distraction.

I left work early that day, soon after Sherry called to tell me the news and I had settled up a morning's worth of sales and had informed the store manager, Mr. Gentry, and Darlene of course that sorrow and the hurt of living had just struck me in a way I had never thought possible. All together it took maybe two hours, including the drive on the freeway, and when I got home the first thing I noticed after giving Sherry a hug and telling her "it'll be all right" was that she had rearranged the furniture in the living room. You can do a lot in two hours. The love seat had traded places with the club chairs. The television was in a new corner and all the tables had been moved. Our old gray sofa bed angled away from its wall, the worn spot on its arm shining up like an ugly lesion I had never really seen before.

Sherry said, "I'll need help with the couch." She looked at me then as if it were all my fault, as if she understood something that she felt free to let me know about now, and there's been a kind of distance, a quiet between us ever since.

They found Gene's body within a week and his name is now listed on government documents under Killed In Action.

As it turned out I stayed with Sherry and Darlene eventually quit her job. She married Mr. Gentry after his first wife passed away and his children moved out of the house. They seem happy and we chat whenever she stops by the store. Mrs. McCarthy never did come back, but once about a month later I saw their rusty pickup sputter by me on the freeway. In the bed of the truck was an old tattered rocking chair rolling back and forth as if a ghost were putting it to use. I chased them down, honked and waved, and she smiled, but her husband speeded up to get away from me.

I hear Sherry calling. She's out in the kitchen ready to go. This evening we're headed off to the new mall to look at a sleek new line of bedroom furniture that my store doesn't carry. I'm planning to retire next year and Sherry's feeling the weight of our ages. We're into the fourth year of what she calls our Complete Home Room by Room Renovation Plan, and her bedroom, Gene's old haunt, is the last one on her list.

EVELINE'S LIZARD

How is it that life can turn on you so simply, so easily, as easily as a lizard changing colors? Such a lizard was clinging to the window screen — Eveline knew him well — and she had watched him change: from that brilliant green, like a child's painting, to that awful, flat, protective brown, the color of old grime and old rust. All her life she had called them chameleons, everyone had. But recently she had read in the *Chronicle* that the proper name of the species was something else. It began with an *a*, a foreign-sounding name. The big lizard puffed himself up and his throat bloomed like a great red flower, a tulip perhaps. She decided to plant tulips under this window, in the spring.

Eveline tamped out her Salem and resettled herself on the dinette chair. The chair had been stationed at the window like a lonely sentry since her first week in the house. Six months already. Every day she sat there for a while and gazed out at the square, yellowing yard, watched the lazy lizards and the ridiculous blue jays, the squirrels, all of whom lived in or under or somewhere near the yard's only tree, a mature tallow in whose trunk someone long ago had hammered boards as a ladder for climbing. The boards were gray now and warped and the nails protruded.

"Mama?" It was Eveline's daughter calling from the living room. Her noisy arrival jarred and abused the little house.

"I'm in here, Nina."

Nina appeared in the doorway of the empty back room. In one arm she held her first, Toby, and in the other a diaper bag. The baby stared at his grandmother as if she were an exotic animal. So did Nina. "What are you doing in here, Mama?"

"Oh, nothing. Thinking. Hello, sweet thing."

Eveline tickled Toby's many chins and wagged her tongue at him. Toby laughed. She could tell that Nina was eyeing her closely, inspecting her face for signs of the trouble. They were both large women, tall and sturdy and heavy in bone structure, the dark-headed, dark-eyed offspring of Scotch-Irish stock who had come to Texas from Tennessee more than a hundred years ago.

"Are you all right, Mama?"

"Yes yes, I'm fine. Come on."

They took Toby into the middle room. Nina and her husband Walter, who together owned the house, had remodeled the room into a fine nursery, bright and airy with shiny mobiles hanging from the ceiling. Eveline put Toby in his crib and fussed over him.

"I'm late, Mama, and I'll be late tonight. Do you mind?"

"Whenever."

"Walter could come by. He wants to talk to you anyway."

"Whatever. Lord knows we'll be here."

On her way out, Nina paused in the short dim hall and straightened the new painting, a still life of peaches and roses that her Aunt Angela had done for her mother as a housewarming present. Nina looked at the painting and frowned — they agreed there was something not quite right about it — and then she frowned at her mother. Eveline anticipated the usual question.

"Yes, I'm fine," her temper said. "Quit staring at me."

Nina smiled tenderly and they kissed and then Nina left for work. From the narrow concrete porch Eveline waved at Nina's new car as it pulled away from the curb, but Nina's thoughts were already far ahead and she didn't look back to see, or to wave.

~

Perhaps the worst was over. This she said to herself every day, and every day she considered praying, thinking it might help like premiums paid on a retirement plan, though she had given up religion long ago, back when things were going so well. The past three years had been an unfortunate time for Eveline Hardesty. No other period of her life had been so "strange," at least not since the day she left her mother's house at the age of seventeen to marry Ed and get away from her family.

But Ed was gone now. That had been the first strange thing.

He was between jobs at the time and one morning about nine o'clock she received a call at the office. He was back in bed; he had a horrible case of indigestion and a severe pain in his arm and he thought maybe he'd go to the doctor. Instead, she told him she would meet him at the hospital and then ordered an ambulance. By the time Eveline arrived at the emergency room he was dead.

Next she lost her job. The company, an import-export

outfit in which she had invested twenty-two years of her life, folded up one day and laid off all its employees. It was the economy, she knew; most everyone in Houston was having a rough time, but she had never really forgiven the owners for going bust.

Over the years they had sent her to night school, promoted her, heaped responsibility on her and raised her salary until, at the end, she held the title of Office Manager and was making almost twice what Ed made as a salesman when he worked. For a woman without a college degree, she had done remarkably well. Her success had given them a comfortable life with two nice cars and a new five-bedroom house on a street called Primrose Avenue. Those were proud, good times. They all felt safe and the future seemed as clear as the past. She and Ed and Nina took a vacation to Europe and they ate out at some of the best restaurants and they always wore new clothes. After college Nina had been hired by a first-rate accounting firm, and Eveline and Ed were doing so well that they helped her buy her first house, the house Nina and Walter and Toby still lived in, though Nina had not met Walter at that time. Never did a day pass, as she recalled it, without Ed telling her that he loved her, and he often came home with gifts. The diamond on her finger, for instance, which Ed presented to her as the engagement ring he had always intended her to have.

For two years Eveline had been searching for work. There had been some offers but in each case the salary was so low that her self-respect forced her to refuse. Now she wished she had taken one of them to tide her over. A large sum of money had been lost when the Primrose Avenue house finally sold and during it all she had lived on her savings. The account was down to a mere $900. Worse yet were the medical bills. One night in April she woke to an explosion of pain in her stomach. She called Nina who sped her to the hospital where the doctors removed her ruptured appendix. A close call, they said; at her age, fifty, she could have died.

She had to rely on Nina and Walter for virtually everything. They paid most of her bills, they fed her, they sometimes took her along when they went out. They had even bought this little house for her to live in until she could get back on her feet. As a kind of payment, she baby-sat for them each day of the week and often on weekends. Eveline knew the house was an investment for them and they had wrangled a great deal on it because of the suffering market. But still, she wanted to pay her own way. She always had.

~

The lizard was back on the screen doing push-ups like an athlete and showing off his red, flowery throat. His body was green again. He looked like a Christmas ornament in the dusky evening light. Eveline was waiting for Nina or Walter to come pick up Toby. She had fed him his supper and put him down again and — what a good baby! — he had gone right off to sleep. Just like his mother, that boy was. Nina had been a sweet child and shy, dependent, having no brothers or sisters, but there was nothing spoiled about her.

"I'm a widow," she said softly, mysteriously. The lizard turned his head and blinked as if wincing at the word.

All of a sudden she saw someone in the yard. It was Walter, still in his suit and tie, his blond hair neatly combed. She liked Walter, who was also an accountant, though he made her nervous with his authoritative ways and too-proper manners, his quiet influence over Nina. He never smiled with his eyes. Walter seemed to be inspecting the tree for something. Eveline called to him through the screen, "Hey, boy, what are you doing?"

He turned, startled, and said, "Oh, hi, Eveline. Didn't mean to startle you. I came in through the gate."

"I know," she said. "How about some coffee?"

At the table in the kitchen Walter sat perfectly straight as if he were attending a formal tea. Eveline, placing a mug in front of him, asked him what he had been up to in the yard. He took a long time to answer, computing the words in his mind.

"We've decided to add on," Walter said. "A den, sort of. It'll give you more space and boost the resale value. Or the rental value. That's way in the future, of course."

"I don't need any more room," said Eveline. "I rattle around in here as it is. And besides you just bought this place."

"We'll have to cut down that tree," he said.

"It's a tallow," she informed him. Eveline looked out the window. In twilight the trunk and limbs, which spread up over the back of the house, looked unreal, as if she were seeing only a memory of the tree. She got up and switched on the back porch lamp. "That would be a shame, Walter. A real shame."

"Got to look to the future," he said and they were silent with each other for a long time until he mentioned that Nina was probably home by then and that he'd better get Toby and go.

Alone, Eveline went out to the back yard. She touched the boards of the ladder, gazed up into the tree's limbs, scanned the dark limbs of all the other trees in the other yards.

"It's not *my* house," she said and went back inside.

~

On Thanksgiving Day Eveline drove up to her sister's

place near Lake Conroe. Angela, twelve years older, had invited her to spend the entire holiday with them. Angela and Floyd's four children were all living elsewhere, so it was just the three of them — "you and the ancient ones," as her sister put it. Though they were only sixty-two, the complaints of age had in fact begun to show on Angela and Floyd. Her sister suffered from high blood pressure and Floyd, who had taken early retirement, still griped of feeling useless; he talked of taking a part-time job to pass the time, "but nobody wants an old poot head." Still, in general, life played on them well. Angela had her painting and her church work, and Floyd had turned the house into a real showplace with his beds of pink azaleas. It was the sort of life Eveline had always hoped she and Ed would have when they retired.

"You should take up painting," Angela said, daubing green onto a canvas to make a pine tree. They were in Angela's "art room." It was Saturday afternoon, the third day of her visit.

"I'm not creative like you," Eveline said from the love seat. She was lying down, letting her leftovers digest and planning a nap. Her feet dangled well beyond the armrest. Through the open window came the intermittent growl of Floyd's Weed-Eater. "You got the imagination and a size eight, I got the strong back and a size fourteen. You got Mama's genes and I got Daddy's. It still amazes me sometimes that Ed had anything to do with me."

Angela turned on her barstool so quickly that she almost upset her easel. She made a quiet, sobbing sound and when Eveline looked over she saw that tears were puddling up and dripping from her eyes. Angela was like that; she cried easily. Her face was contorted and sweet and in such anguish that she had the look of a very old child in a grown-up's smock.

"What is it, hun?" Eveline hefted herself off the couch and hugged her sister, bending over. Their eyeglasses clinked.

"I just . . . I hate to hear you talk about yourself like that. You're too honest sometimes."

"Why? There was nothing wrong with Daddy. He was just big and kind of ugly. Mother was the problem. Never lifted a single pretty finger all her life. You're lucky you overcame it."

"You can do anything you want," Angela sniffled. "You're so smart. God provides, and we can help. Move up here with us."

"I don't need your help. I'm doing fine."

"Careful, here comes Floyd."

Eveline had noticed nothing, no indicators that Floyd was in the house, but suddenly there he stood in the hall. Floyd was the same height as Eveline with white hair and a moustache, very distinguished in appearance. Beads of sweat had smeared his dirty face and in his hands was the Weed-Eater. He appeared angry.

"Have you been using this thing?"

Angela shook her head no.

"Yes, you have. It's all fouled up. I can't keep it running." He pulled the crank a few times but the Weed-Eater only sputtered and spit out oil. He glared at Angela. "How many times have I told you: you leave the outside to me and I'll gladly leave the inside to you. Don't mess with what you don't understand." He glared at her again and left in a flourish. Angela whispered, "I just used it to trim up my garden spot out back. Since he retired, he won't trim my garden spot."

Floyd was in a sour humor all night but by Sunday morning he had recovered and he even apologized — to Eveline, not to Angela. Eveline never knew how to take

Floyd. He made her angry over the way he intimidated Angela, and she knew that he had never approved of Ed's easy attitude toward work and money (Floyd had been a banker, after all). But he'd gone out of his way to be kind to Eveline since Ed's death and he had agreed eagerly to give away the bride in Ed's place when Nina and Walter married.

"A person needs to be occupied," Floyd was saying. "An idle mind will kill you quicker than anything."

Angela had convinced Eveline to go to church with her that morning. While Angela was dressing, Floyd, in his banker's tone of voice, kept asking Eveline questions about her financial position and prospects for employment. Eveline had the feeling she was being interviewed for a loan application, even though Floyd was still in his robe; he didn't go to church anymore.

"Well, there is this one job," she said. "I applied and they called to see if I was still available, but I don't know if they'll call back. It's the same kind of work I did before."

"That's good. . . ." Floyd seemed hesitant. "Have you thought about doing temporary work? You know, typing or filing. A widow can't be too choosy. In fact, I know a man — "

"No, I really haven't," Eveline interrupted. "Have you?"

Just then Angela bustled in talking about the "glorious morning" and how it was "just perfect for the Lord's work." Floyd rolled his eyes. Angela said, "Come on, girl, our preacher hates for you to be late. Here, I brought your purse."

The church was just a few miles away. It was all brick and looked less like a church than a real estate office with its simple peaked roof, square windows and raised sign out front. What's more, the preacher was young and over-dressed and he even concluded his sermon with a real estate metaphor: "Sign on the dotted line, brothers and sisters, close your deal for God. Come on down with your voices." Once the congregation had lifted to its feet and stirred up the hymn, Angela grabbed Eveline by the hand and pulled her into the aisle. "Get your purse," she whispered.

"What are you doing?"

"You'll see," said Angela and then she led Eveline to the front of the church and into the hands of the smiling preacher.

"My little sister would like to place membership."

"No, Angela," Eveline whispered but it was too late.

The preacher put them on the front pew. He gave her a pen and an index card with some questions typed on it. Eveline looked at Angela with exasperation, but Angela's face was so aglow with her good work that all Eveline could do was start writing.

When the hymn ended, the preacher took the card from Eveline and, reading from it, introduced her to the congregation in joyful tones. Then he said, "Let us pray."

Eveline tried to listen, but his lofty words seemed too lofty for the occasion and they embarrassed her, so she shut out his voice and attempted a prayer of her own. It was no good; nothing would form in her mind. And with startling clarity it came to her why. She didn't believe in God anymore. The God of her childhood, Angela's God, wouldn't allow life to turn on you so completely, wouldn't allow you to fall so far. She felt sorry for her sister, placing all her hope in an innocent dream of the future, and she felt sorry for herself too, having lost such hope. As the preacher continued in his soft, gentle voice, tears of self-pity and shame crept into Eveline's eyes. So she opened her purse for a Kleenex. And that's when she found the check, tucked into a side pocket. It was made out to Eveline Hardesty and she had to blink six times before she could believe all those zeroes. A thousand dollars. At the bottom was Floyd's signature and on the MEMO line was written, "Loan." She glanced at Angela, but her sister's eyes were closed in prayer. Eveline snapped shut her purse and wiped her tears with a finger.

"Go out, all of you, and do God's business," the preacher said after his "Amen," and the congregation rose to its feet.

~

To avoid a scene, Eveline waited until Monday to return the check. Angela hadn't said a word about the money; she must have talked Floyd into it and then wanted it to be a surprise for Eveline when she got home.

That afternoon, while she was changing Toby's diapers, the man with the job called again. He said he was setting up interviews. Would next Monday fit into her schedule? She said, "Just a second." She smiled and said, "Yes, it would."

Eveline was so thrilled she could hardly breathe. It had been two months since her last interview and this man sounded serious. She knew better than to tell anyone. But that evening when Nina arrived she couldn't contain her excitement; her face was hot with it.

"You look like somebody just gave you a thousand dollars," Nina said, lifting Toby onto her hip. "What's up?"

"It's going to be a good Christmas. I can feel it."

On Friday morning a man with a clipboard came to the house. He said Walter had sent him to do an appraisal of what the add-on would cost. "That tree'll have to go," he said.

"It's a tallow," Eveline informed him.

She called Nina at her office.

"Are y'all really going to cut down my tallow tree?"

"We'll plant others."

"It won't be the same. I'll be dead and buried by the time they're as big as this one. Couldn't you wait a month or so?"

"Walter wants to do it this year. For tax purposes."

"I'll pay the taxes."

"It's not a matter of paying them, it's a matter of deducting them. You know that. . . . Listen, I got to go."

Eveline was silent on the line. She had hoped that if she got this job, any job, she would be able to buy the house from Walter and Nina and save the tree. She didn't need a den.

Nina said, "Are you all right . . . Eveline?"

"Eveline?"

"It was Walter's idea. He thinks I should quit with 'Mama.'"

∼

The interview went smoothly. It was the perfect job for her with a large, secure company based in San Francisco. She would, more or less, pick up just where she had left off. She talked briefly with two men in their separate offices. Then they took her to lunch. The three of them got along like old friends.

"With your experience we see a cost savings to the company of several thousand dollars. We want you at the first of the year, and we'll project the move to San Francisco by Feb-First."

"Wait a minute," said Eveline. "San Francisco?"

The two men, both shorter than Eveline, and younger and brighter and busier, looked at each other. "Didn't you tell her?" They laughed and reddened. "Sorry," said one. "We've talked to so many," said the other. "It's being transferred to headquarters after training here with us. That decision delayed the hire."

"I sure thought you knew," said the balding redhead.

"Is that a problem?" said the blond. "Relocating?"

"Yes," she said. "I mean, no. I love San Francisco."

They wanted her answer by Christmas.

Eveline drove home in confusion. In her previous job she had traveled all over the States and to six foreign countries, but she had lived all her life in Houston. She couldn't imagine living anywhere else. Everything about her was associated with the city. What about Nina? (She'd never allow it.) And Toby? What about Angela? Who would visit Ed's grave? And she didn't know a soul in San Francisco, or in all of California for that matter.

Two trucks were parked in front of the house. On the doors of each was a sign: Mackey's Tree Service. She went inside, paid the elderly lady from next door for watching Toby, ushered her out in a hurry and then stepped to the back door. Limbs and branches and yellow berries were strewn all over the yard. Three men were sitting on the ground, taking a coffee break, it appeared. The trunk of the tallow tree was already naked as a toothpick. She went to her bedroom to change out of her good clothes. She heard a chain saw crank up outside. She sat down on the bed in nothing but her underwear. She just listened. . . .

~

Christmas was the finest time of the year to Eveline. Houston's humid weather usually turned for good in December and the holiday brought to mind the only really good memories she had of her childhood, of her father bringing home the tree and her mother baking rich-smelling pies in the kitchen. It was a longstanding tradition that Eveline and her family would gather at Angela's house for the annual celebration on Christmas Eve. This year, and with only a week to go, no one had called to set-

tle plans and recently Nina never had time to talk.
Eveline knew the holidays were the hardest time on people alone and more than ever before she was looking forward to the get-together up in Conroe. She decided to
make the arrangements herself.

"I've been meaning to tell you for weeks," Angela said
over the phone. Then she started crying. "We're going to
Kansas City for Christmas." It was Floyd's idea to meet in
Missouri at the home of the eldest son, because "it's more
central, geographically speaking, you know," Angela said,
sniffling.

"Hush now," said Eveline. "It's not the end of the
world."

"Plan on coming up for New Year's, hun, will you?"

When Nina arrived that evening Eveline broke the
news and suggested an alternative. "Why don't we all have
Christmas here. Maybe you could invite some friends.
We'll have a real party."

Nina said just what Angela had said: "I've been meaning to tell you for weeks." They were going skiing.

"Skiing? You don't know how to ski."

"We can learn, Mama. Eveline. Heard of ski instructors?"

"You don't have to be smart with me. . . ."

"What about Toby?"

Nina's face answered the question. "Please, Mama?"

"It's Eveline." Eveline gave her daughter a sarcastic
look.

Nina said, "I mean, Eveline."

"I'll have to think about it," her mother said. "Turns out
I've got some news of my own. A job offer."

She hadn't intended to tell Nina until she had made
the decision. She knew it would complicate things; Nina
would be upset and irrational about it. But Eveline was
tired of being the only one with no developments in her

life. Now it had slipped out, more like a confession than an announcement.

"Tell me why I shouldn't go," said Eveline.

Oddly, Nina's reaction was mixed. She was excited about the offer but hesitant to advise Eveline to move. It would be such a startling change. They had never lived so far apart from each other. "You have to think of your family," she said at one point. By the time she had packed up Toby, however, Nina's position had softened. The salary, the benefits, the opportunities: a career requires sacrifices, she said. "I mean, we could visit back and forth several times a year. And just think — San Francisco."

"So, you're saying I ought to do it?" Eveline heard the surprise in her voice which rose from the surprise in her heart.

"I don't know, Mama. It may be for the best. You need to get on with your life. Daddy would want you to, don't you think?"

They went silent and thoughtful and their eyes wandered.

Eveline said, "How much rent will y'all ask for this place?"

"Walter thinks we could get four hundred," said Nina who immediately realized her mistake. "Oh, Mama, that has nothing to do with it."

"I know, I know," Eveline said. "Close your mouth."

"Well, it doesn't. I'd never. . . ."

Nina's protest was so vehement that Eveline could hear Walter's plans for the future in every word. And she knew that Walter was right. And Floyd too.

"Here, give me a kiss and go on home to your husband."

That night Eveline bought her Christmas tree and then went shopping at the mall. Everyone in the crowd seemed to be with someone else and they were all carrying packages. The familiar music put her in a queer, distant mood. She couldn't smile at anyone or anything, until, in a little boutique, she came across something that was just perfect for her tree. It was a Christmas ornament in the shape of a lizard. The glass was all green except for a crescent of red at the throat. It reminded her that she hadn't seen the real lizard in more than a week, not since the day before Walter's hired men had hacked down her beautiful tallow, the lizard's home. And that reminded her that the men were coming on Monday to start work on the add-on. Everything would be disrupted, dusty and noisy, for no telling how long.

She bought the ornament, but when she got home, instead of hanging it on the tree, she attached it to the window screen in the empty back room, hoping it would entice the real lizard to return. Eveline knew it was a false whim, a doubtful idea, at least until the construction work was done and everything was back to normal, which might not occur until well after New Year's, and she realized then that she might never see the lizard again.

Suddenly she said, "I'm a widow, I tell you, as if you didn't know." Her voice echoed within the empty room. In a rush of temper she snatched the ornament from the window screen, snapping the flimsy piece of wire she had attached it with. She hurried into the living room and carelessly hung the thing on the tree, where it belonged. It dangled from its limb all alone, green on green, still swaying from her heavy touch.

"I'm a widow," she said again, but softly, mysteriously this time, and she finally heard the truth in it.

THE WONDROUS
NATURE
OF REPENTANCE

We were religious in the worst of ways then and looked at things differently than most people, more severely, or more biblically maybe — everything we did involved The Church — and Father ruled with a cast-iron hand. Back in his deacon days.

I was only eight when all this happened, so I don't know for sure. But this is what I remember and what I've figured from them since — them being Mother and Jancy (Jancy's my sister, only two years older, almost in college now) and Roger (my brother by nine years, a real flesh-and-blood brother) and there was Brother Hobson (the preacher at church) and there was Father too, though he hates to talk about it.

So here's what happened. It was Sunday. First, all four of the kittens died and then Roland (he's my brother by ten years, the oldest of us, my favorite) and Roland's wife who was his girlfriend then — or maybe his fiancee already, or maybe she was his wife already. Anyway, the kittens died and then Roland and Mary went down front to confess before the whole congregation. Not over the kittens, I know that now. They confessed their love, as best I can tell, which must have been an awful sin, as it got everybody in an uproar. A terrible time. And then they had the wedding. And I became Uncle Robert. And then everybody simmered down, even Father, and everything changed. But that was later, after Tiger and Roland had both left home.

For me it begins with Tiger, our cat that we'd had a long time, maybe a year, ever since old Max the dog had run away.

Jancy and I named her Tiger because of her stripes and because she was fierce and independent too, a real tomcat we thought, though we might have named her something else like Sophie or Elsie if we'd known. I guess nobody who could have told us different had ever looked, being so busy and so tall you know, and mostly ignoring the cat anyway since Mother had made it clear that she was to be our responsibility and ours alone, Jancy and me, "not like the dog that I ended up caring for despite your promises." And so we didn't find out the truth till one day after school when Mother said, "What's wrong with Tiger?"

The cat was all bloated like a toad and she'd been whining all afternoon and wandering through the house as if searching for something she'd lost. Jancy and I didn't think much of it till Mother said, "What's wrong with Tiger?" and she got that curious smile on her pretty face, young face then, a look like she'd just got a wonderful surprise. Mother stooped and hugged us to her and we leaned over Tiger who was crying and staring up at us from the floor with an air about her like she'd sat down on an ice cube.

Mother said, "Tiger, I'm afraid, my little lovelies — oh, my goodness" (and she grinned at us then like we'd done something precious) — "Tiger," she said, "is about to be a mother."

"No," said Jancy.

"Oh, yes," said Mother. "I'm afraid so. And any minute now it appears." Then her eyes went serious, kind of perplexed-looking, the same expression that was in Jancy's eyes, and Mother said, sort of to herself, "I can't believe I didn't notice."

Tiger lived out back in the garage most of the time. But we made her a bed of an old blanket and a cardboard box and put it in the washroom, because Mother said it would be better.

When Father came home and we told him (Jancy got to him first before he even had a chance to put down his briefcase, but she jumbled it up, so I said, "Tiger's having babies," and Mother just stood there nodding) he went to the washroom and squatted down and petted Tiger quite gently, which was odd for Father who never paid the cat any attention. And he said, "Hello there, old boy — old girl, I guess now. Just full of surprises." Then he said, "And not even married."

"Do cats get married, Daddy?" I asked but he just chuckled and squeezed my head.

Then Roger came home from Bible study and he went to look at Tiger and then Roland came in from Debate Club and he went in to look, and at dinner everyone was happy and expectant. Roland said, "Hey, Robby, you a girl or a boy?" and then he winked all around the table and Roger laughed at me and Father chuckled, until Mother said, "Roland, hush! All of you, hush!" But she was teasing too. "I promise you he's a boy." At that Roland gave another wink, just for me, and I felt better.

In the morning there was magic. The box was full of kittens crawling all around Tiger and chewing on her belly and making the craziest noises, and Mother looked very tired. So did Tiger.

"Was Tiger bad?" asked Jancy, which seemed like a good question to me, though I hadn't thought about it. But Mother said, "No, of course not. What gave you such an idea?"

Jancy shrugged and Mother looked at me and I shrugged too.

That was a Wednesday. I remember because that night we went to prayer meeting, which we did every Wednesday back then. After the singing and after Brother Hobson preached his sermon and it was time to pray, I asked God to watch out for the kittens. I guess he didn't hear for all the other prayers coming up to him at that moment, or maybe it was something else. . . .

Anyway, in the car on the way home Mother and Father argued about Roland who was not with us that night. This was the first whimper of the uproar.

Father said, "I don't see why he can't attend, what with me a deacon and all."

"You know perfectly well why. He's a grown man now and about to graduate and he and Mary have things to do."

"I know that," he said. "I know that. But I have to wonder just what sorts of things." Then he called back to Roger, "What's your brother up to tonight?"

At that time Roger wanted to be a minister and he stayed to himself except for Bible study and he was mostly quiet except when he was talking about Jesus, and he and Roland didn't always get along. But he said, "Senior Boys' Club, I think."

Father said, "So he's out carousing. . . ."

"Oh, Richard!" said Mother.

"I don't know what he's doing," said Roger.

Father said, "And what about Mary?"

"I don't know," said Roger who hated arguments.

Father looked at Mother. "It was a mistake, you letting him buy that car," he said.

"He's a good boy," Mother said.

"But how does it look? With me a deacon and all. And her own father a deacon as well. Don't you know that people talk."

"They're good children," Mother said.

Jancy spoke up then: "Mother, is a deacon like a disciple in the Bible?" and I looked toward her voice in the dark back seat. "A rhyme," I said and I thought it was only to myself, but Mother and Father looked at each other and then they glanced back at Roger and for some reason all three of them started laughing.

Then Tiger moved the kittens. It was a few days later, a Saturday, the day of the prom that Roland and Mary went to but didn't come home from that night, or the next morning either.

Anyway, that day Tiger was sort of fidgety and nervous and then about lunch time we saw her out back pacing across the yard. She was toting one of the kittens in her mouth. She went into the garage and by the time Jancy and I got out there she was already up among the rafters. This is how we found her regular home, where she stayed when she wasn't in the house or out catting around. It was in the hollow part of the eaves. Jancy crawled up on the table saw and then up higher onto the lathe so she could see. "Golly," she hollered. "It's just like a nest in here."

So then Tiger brought out the last kitten. She jumped down from the rafters and slunk back across the yard and

entered the house through the little dog door in the big
door, Max's old door. We followed her again, and Father
and Mother came too, and when we looked up sure
enough there was one of the kittens just hanging over the
edge, pawing the air. And sure enough it stepped off, but
quick as anything Tiger's big head shot out and she
snatched the kitten back at the very instant it fell.

Mother said, "Richard, perhaps we should bring them
down."

"No no," Father said. "It's only natural. We don't want
to tamper with something like this."

That afternoon Roland dressed himself up in a tuxedo.
Then he left in his car. It was an old Dodge, a '54 convert-
ible with flames on the sides that he'd saved for working
summers at Mr. Hardessey's lumberyard. I had been out
hunting jays with my BB gun and was up in the big tallow
tree where he couldn't see me, and I watched him. He
primped a bit in the rearview and then he cranked her up.
But before starting off he leaned over and took something
out of the glove box. He glanced all around as though to
see if anybody was out, and then, just like that, he lit up a
cigarette. He blew out a whirl of smoke and with only one
hand on the wheel he drove away, looking for all the
world like a grown-up on TV, or a spy in the movies. So I
had a secret on Roland.

Then Roland came home again. Mary was with him.
And she was so pretty in her pink, fluffy dress and her hair
all made up that I could feel my face burning whenever I
looked at her. There was something different about her, in
her eyes, like the eyes of the ladies you see in magazines,
the ones wearing just petticoats. I couldn't help sneaking
looks at her, even though I had known her most of my life,
and knew her parents, and knew her brother and her sister
as if we were all cousins. So I had another secret.

Father and Mother made a big hubbub over Mary, and Roger took a book's worth of pictures. First, with them outside by the boxwoods before the light went, and then inside with Mary sitting in a living room chair, and then with Roland standing beside Mary, and then three or four of Roland pinning on the flower as everybody joked about how he couldn't find enough material to pin it to, and even Father turned red in the face then.

"You're both so . . . so beautiful," Mother said. "Mary so pretty and Roland so handsome. Why, you look like the Kennedys, like Jack and Jackie." Everybody laughed. Then she said, "It's no wonder — " but that was as far as she got before the tears started up and so Father hugged her and sure enough Roger snapped a picture of that too. And then Roland and Mary left again. We all watched at the windows. Father stood there a long time, long after they had driven away, till Mother called him in to dinner.

Then came the uproar. It went on for weeks.

Sunday morning when we got up Mother and Father were arguing. Or at least Father was arguing. I could tell that Mother was sitting there in the kitchen just taking it. From the hall I heard Father say, "I expected him to get home late, that's understandable. But this is going too far."

So Mother said, "Richard, for heaven's sake, all the kids do it. It's sort of a rite, a tradition."

"That's fine for them," said Father. "But we aren't these other people and I won't have it. Just how will it look?"

"It won't look like anything," Mother said, and then there was a pause and I could tell just by the silence, the length of it and the stillness, that Father was giving her the glare. It lasted till Mother said, "Don't do that to me, Richard."

"And you refuse to call the Zimmermans?" he said, meaning Mary's parents. And Mother said, "It's not that I refuse. I just don't see the point. If they're worried, they'll call us."

I decided to make my entrance. Father stopped in mid-sentence when he saw me and he gave me the glare too. Mother jumped up and started breakfast and Father poured himself more coffee and he just stood there in his robe, sipping it, his hair all balled up on his head the way it always did when worry wouldn't let him keep his hands still. Then here came Jancy and she said just the wrong thing: "Where's Roland?"

Father flew all over her, saying, "We won't be speaking of Roland. Sit down here, young lady, and eat your breakfast." At which Jancy twisted up her face like she was about to wail, so Mother made a big fuss over her, giving Father mean glances.

Roger came in then and Father must have changed his mind. Because right off he started in on him about Roland. But all Roger did was shrug and say I don't know.

"Well, at least one of you has the sense to behave the way we raised you," Father said, meaning Roger who never got into trouble. "Perhaps your brother and Mary would like to take up residence together, like beatniks, or whatever they're called."

And Mother said, "Richard, that's enough."

Father got loud then, ranting about how it wasn't enough and wouldn't be enough till Roland was home and explained himself. He went on for quite a while. In fact we could hear him all the time we were dressing for church. It made me not want to speak to Father and so I asked Roger for help with my bow tie.

We didn't go to Sunday school that day and in the car Father had made it clear he wanted us all together and that we would be leaving, pronto, right after the service. Which we did. He marched us out to the car as soon as the closing prayer was said and he put us inside and then he went away for a few minutes. I could see him on the lawn of the church talking to a couple of the other deacons, Brother Murtry, his boss at the company, and Brother Evans that Mother called the richest man she had ever known. Father was frowning when he came back to the car.

On the way home he told Mother that he had also talked to the Zimmermans. He said *they* were worried to *death* and would call if they heard something. He gave Mother the glare again. I was getting kind of sick over the way he was acting, and since there was no place I could go to hide, and I couldn't think of anything else to do, I started singing. It just came out of me, that kids' song about how Jesus loves the little children, and I got louder and louder on each verse, and then Jancy started in with me, and Mother glanced back with an encouraging smile — not a smile really, but eyes that said *Yes, yes, that's right* — and then I heard her voice singing too, and then Roger too. All of us singing *red and yellow, black and white* and so forth.

Which really touched off Father who suddenly stopped the car beside the road and got out. He said to Mother, "I'm walking home." But we all kept singing. He walked up the road about half a block and stopped, and other cars were driving by and people were gawking at us. Father stood there for a minute with his hands in his pockets like he didn't know what was what and then quick as a lizard he kicked a stone into the ditch and came back, looking furious with us. That's when we quit singing.

Roland's Dodge was parked in front of the house and he was in his bed when we went inside. All I heard from Father was "Where have you been?" before Mother grabbed Jancy and me. She fed us alone in the kitchen and then she sent us out to play.

Tiger was up in the garage and the little kittens were all just peeking over the edge or walking hazardously among the joists. Jancy said they were almost weaned, but I didn't know what she was talking about. "That's when they leave the nest," she told me. "Mother says it's an awful time."

That afternoon Roland went away. Mother said he was staying with his best friend Freddy Mathews. Jancy asked, "Is Roland being weaned?" but Mother just looked sad and hugged us both.

In the house then, and for days afterward, there was all kinds of discussing going on between Mother and Father and even Roger. After Roland came home they would sit with him in the living room for long stretches, talking in low voices, though sometimes they got loud and Roland would stomp off to his room. In the second week things smoothed over. We ate supper at the regular time and Mother and Father seemed to be themselves again. School was out. Roger went away to a church retreat in the country and Roland was working at the lumberyard.

About that time Tiger brought the kittens down from the rafters. They'd scramble all over the yard and Tiger would just lie there like a queen, ignoring them. Everything caught their attention, especially the car, the Chevy. They would crawl onto the tires and up under the hood and Jancy and I would have to dig them out. They were too ignorant to be afraid, I guess, even of the roaring engine, so that Mother got to where she wouldn't even start her up without checking to see they were gone.

But that morning, that Sunday morning, because we were in a hurry, or because Roland was driving us and because Mother had other things on her mind maybe, nobody checked.

We got into the car, the Chevy, Roland and Father in

the front, and Mother between Jancy and me in the back. Father and Roland were talking, and Mother was retying Jancy's bow, quite normal, and then Roland cranked her up and slipped her into gear and he put his arm up on the seat, peering back, and I felt the car starting backwards and I felt something, something in the simple first movement of the car or in Roland's concentrated gaze that went over us and beyond us, or just something that told me this was wrong — something made me yell, "Wait! Stop!" And Roland slammed on the brakes. It was then that we heard the scream.

Roland's look was all shock and already his eyes were apologizing, and frightened too. Mother said, "Oh, no," and she was over me and out the door before anybody else could act. All four of the kittens were dead, three crushed by the tires and one caught in the fan belt, the little bodies all bloody and twisted but perfectly calm. Father sent me inside to get shoe boxes.

He said, "Our closet," meaning his and Mother's. "Jancy, you go help him. Go! Quickly."

In the back of the closet, under the old smell of their old clothes, we found plenty of shoe boxes. I had known they were there, knew all along, knew that Mother had saved them for something just like this. Father was waiting for us at the door. "Stay here," he said. He took the boxes and went off behind the garage. It was just a minute before he emerged and waved to us to come.

Roland worked the shovel there by Mother's compost pile. Mother was holding his suit coat over her arm. On the ground sat the four boxes — two from Thom McAn, one from Penny's and one just plain. Then Father put the boxes in the hole that Roland had dug and Roland covered them with dirt and Mother hugged us to her, Jancy and me, and we all prayed. I peeked and saw Tiger sitting by herself out in the yard just licking her paws like this had nothing to do with her.

So we got in the car again, everybody quiet as midnight, and we set out again for church, even though we were quite late. About halfway, on the road by the railroad tracks, Roland stopped the car, just as Father had done. His face looked horrible, confused and fearful and sad. He said, "I've got to think. Y'all go on," and with that he was out the door. Father yelled to him to wait, to come back, but Mother said to let him go, and he did.

We had missed Sunday school and Brother Hobson was already well under way with his sermon, so half the congregation of maybe 500 people glanced over their shoulders at us when we slipped in and sat down under the balcony. It was about fifteen minutes later before Roland appeared. His shirt was unbuttoned and his tie was down and he looked like he had run all the way. He hurried up the side aisle to the pew where he and Mary always sat, and right off they started whispering, Roland with his arm around her on the pewback. Mary's head would turn so her ear was to his mouth and then her head would turn so her mouth was to his ear, and then Mother and Father started whispering back and forth above Jancy and me. Each time they said something they would slide a little closer together and their hips would push Jancy and me along with them until I was almost sitting on Jancy's lap.

This went on till Roland and Mary got up and walked out, holding hands and going quickly, as if what they had to say to each other was too important for whispers. I think everybody in the church watched them leave and old Brother Hobson paused in his sermon as if he'd lost his place, and even he watched until the door to the foyer closed behind Roland and Mary.

Then the uproar became a rage.

It was at the end of the sermon. We were all standing and singing that hymn about how softly and tenderly Jesus calls us, and there was Brother Jones, our song leader, up in the pulpit now and waving his hand, his mouth round and gleeful. And there was Brother Hobson on the steps in front of the pulpit with his Bible raised high, calling the sinners down front to confess in prayer before us all, and his voice rang loud and beseeching above our singing. It wasn't going too well for old Brother Hobson as nobody had taken the step, and we were singing extra verses of the hymn just in case somebody who needed to was hesitating. Everybody was glancing around as they sang to see who might do it. And that's when they did it.

Mary came first, walking down the center aisle with tears rolling from her eyes and looking directly at Brother Hobson, who was looking directly at her, too, with a face that showed surprise as if she were the last person in creation he expected to see. We had reached the end of the hymn for about the third or fourth time and so Brother Hobson turned and nodded to Brother Jones and Brother Jones threw up his hand again and set us off singing yet another verse. Brother Hobson came down from the steps and took Mary's hand and smiled at her warmly and knowingly and directed her to a seat on the front pew and then he stepped away, gazing hopefully up the center aisle again.

So Roland came second. Only he came quickly as if he wanted to catch up with Mary, or get away from something. Now none of us had ever gone down front before, what with Father a deacon and all. And I could feel heat all through my body, knowing how people would act toward us in the future, how they would smile at us wretchedly as if we were sick, the same way Mother and Father always smiled at people who'd confessed. Father said, "Roland, no!" and he started toward the aisle as if he wanted to grab Roland and bring him back. But Mother reached out for him, held him there, and they looked at each other with faces of ruin.

Brother Hobson took Roland's hand and sat him down next to Mary and then he looked up the aisle one more time just in case there was anybody left. Mother and Father went to whispering again till the singing quit and we sat down with everybody coughing and shuffling and arranging themselves, and Father's eyes were very grave. Jancy said, "What are they doing, Mama?" but Mother just shook her head.

Brother Hobson talked then about the wondrous nature of repentance and how God loves us all and forgives us all no matter what, and then we prayed for the sinners, who weren't sinners at all: they were Roland and Mary. And we sang another song and prayed again and then finally it was over and we started filing out, all the brothers and sisters smiling and chattering and shaking hands as if nothing in the world had happened.

But something had happened, at least to us, and Father couldn't get out of there fast enough. He took us straight to the car and then went off in search of Roland. He came back in just a few minutes looking wretched and saying he couldn't find Roland and that we were leaving without him. Which we did.

Roland was waiting for us at home. He explained that Freddy Mathews had driven him in his car. Father said, "I hope you know what you've done to us," and there was lots of low-voice talking again. Jancy and I were sent outside, of course. We looked all over the garage and the yard but couldn't find Tiger anywhere and we never saw her again after that day.

The sun had dried out the patch of ground where the

kittens were buried behind the garage. Jancy knelt and
smoothed out the little balls of dried dirt on top as if she
were sweeping the floor with her hand and then she stuck
four sticks in the ground like crosses. We just stood there
for a while looking at the balls of dried dirt and the sticks
and I imagined the little kitten bodies in their shoe
boxes — calm and peaceful but gone forever and forever
changed. Jancy said, "Poor Roland — but why Mary?" and
this got me to thinking and then to praying the way
Mother had taught us, as I knew I would never have the
courage to go down front and confess, and I didn't know
any better then.

"Oh, Lord," I said. "Please forgive me for the blue jay I
killed with my BB gun and please forgive me for the garter
snake I sliced in two with the hoe last week and please forgive me for the toad I smashed with the rock that time
down in the creek. . . ."

But that was all I could remember of the killing I had
done in my life, and besides Mother was calling us in for
lunch.

IN AN
ARID
LAND

W hat I'm about to tell took place near the little town of Alpine, Texas, when I was fresh out of the service and had some money in my pockets, the first real sum of money I'd ever come across, though looking back I see it was just a pittance in an expensive world, and I had what I thought then was a lot of time ahead of me. The thing that happened shouldn't have happened and I wish that it never did. But there's no denying it and in a way I've been on the lam because of it ever since.

I'll call myself John, as good a name as any, and I should make it clear that I've changed quite a bit over the years. I have a wife now and two children, plus my sister's girl to help out, and I own a business that's done pretty well by us these past few years. We live on a piece of land outside the town of Huntsville, Texas, with enough acreage to graze a few cows and to keep our two horses. And we have friends there who know nothing about me except that I give money to the local Democrats, and take my kids to church on Sundays, and help out my neighbors when I can. This is the way a man should live, the sort of life that keeps you out of trouble. It's a happier life than others.

Of course that's not easy to know when you're twenty-one and full of the stuff the Marine Corps pumps into you — the stuff time has not yet had the opportunity to pump out again. I'm talking now of 1974 when the war was slowing down and Nixon had been found out, people still wore bell-bottom jeans, and possession of even a few marijuana seeds was a thirty-year crime in Texas.

I received my discharge the Monday after Halloween at the base in California and I took a bus to Alpine to spend some time with my big sister Marie and her little girl Crissy. Our folks were long since dead, so these two were all the family I had and I guess I was wanting to make that kind of contact again. I was also looking forward to some good times at some bars that weren't full of guys wearing khaki or olive drab, and I knew that Marie's husband — I'll call him David Smith — I knew David could be counted on to point these out. I say husband, but far as I know there was no marriage license on file in any courthouse anywhere. From what I could tell in her letters they had lived together long enough and cared enough about each other that one day they simply started calling themselves married. He was "Daddy" to little Crissy, whose natural father had died in a copter crash on a rig in the Gulf before she was even born. This was back when I was a freshman in high school, after Marie had left home and school at seventeen and taken up with a pretty rough crowd of oil-field people and fliers down in Corpus Christi. In some regards David wasn't much different from those people but at least he was kind to them and helped provide for them when he could.

I had met David only once, when I was on leave in Houston — just after boot camp for me and before they moved to Alpine hoping the high-desert air might help little Crissy's bad lungs — and he had kept me drunk and stoned for the better part of a week before putting me on a flight back to San Diego. David had been to college and he'd been in the war too, long before my time, as a pilot of light observation planes. But he got into some kind of trouble with his higher-ups. There was a court martial involved, a bit of prison time, some nasty business with a rotten bed sheet and a light fixture that wouldn't hold his weight, and frightful nightmares plagued him the rest of his life. This is all Marie ever told me about it, and I could see how he and the military would not get along. Still, to hear Marie talk, he could fly a plane as if he'd been born with a control stick in his hand. But then pilots and aircraft had always turned Marie's head. She liked to ride low and fast, all the while swearing that what she really wanted was "the chance to own my own place and to raise my own tomatoes." At least that's what she talked about in her letters back then and for all I know she's searching for it to this day. A sadness comes over me whenever I think of her.

~

I remember the morning I arrived in Alpine as one of the best of my life. The bus ride had been an all-nighter and I hadn't slept for thinking about what was up ahead. So I was awake for the sunrise, which is quite a sight in West Texas and quite a feeling too, what with the nights so black and deep that you have to wonder if daylight will ever come again.

On our way south from the interstate we had passed by

the Davis Mountains where my old Dad used to take me camping in the woods near the observatory — we lived in Odessa then, one of several oil towns I knew pretty well by the time I was twelve and we settled in Houston — and those mountains were perhaps my favorite place in the world. A mass of swirling purple clouds hung low on the peaks and I imagined the storm that was forming up there and I wanted to be in it, sleeping in a tent or just driving a pickup with the wipers slapping across the windshield. This was the feeling I had for the mountains. But more than all that I was a civilian again, thinking civilian thoughts for the first time in three years, and when I stepped off that bus it was like being in a new country.

Marie was waiting for me at the depot, all kisses and hugs. She was thin as a cedar stay and her hair had gone from blonde to that muddy color blondes go. She was still smoking cigarettes like they were the breath of life itself. Right off I noticed the odor of food all over her, and when I told her she smelled like she'd just stepped out of the kitchen, she said, "Well, I have. I'm working these days in the cafeteria over at the college. In fact, I got to hustle you home and get on back to work."

In the truck she told me that Crissy was in school and David was at the house. "He's real nervous about seeing you," she said. "It's some kind of business deal. He says soldier boys always get out with a load of cash and he wants to talk you out of some of yours. For the good of us all, he says."

Marie looked at me like she wanted me to commit to something, so I asked her what it was and she said she didn't know, "exactly," which was a lie plain enough, and then we talked of other matters as she drove us out of town.

She told me how she hated her job and how, though he

had a knack for coming up with money, it seemed David could never find anything but temporary work, and how Crissy had grown tall like her daddy but hadn't outgrown the problem with her lungs, and how that afternoon she would have to leave work again to take Crissy to a doctor's appointment. She told me all kinds of things. And I had that uneasy feeling you get when you arrive some place and realize that the people have been living on their own all the time you've been gone without pausing to wait for you, and that you've waded into something that's like a swiftly moving river full of water and debris that have come from far away. We were easy with each other, telling stories and catching up, but when we rolled into the yard her eyes cut to me and held on. She smiled like a sister. She touched my arm. Her fingers rubbed the material of my uniform and then she squeezed my hand, and she looked as happy to have me as I was to be there.

The house was small but sturdy, with stone walls and a tin roof, an old ranch house that the owner rented to them for next to nothing. She said it was a bargain David had made for some work he did. Out back a stand of mesquites shaded a barbecue pit and a Honda motorcycle that was under repair. Toys and tools were all around. On the kitchen table waited two buckets of Kentucky Fried Chicken and hanging from tape between them was a paper napkin with WELCOME HOME JOHNNY BOY printed on it in red crayon. Under the table lay old Shepherd Fred who didn't move except to thump his tail when Marie spoke his name out of habit and a natural politeness that extended even to dogs and bums.

"I'm afraid it's not much of a party," she said. "But I remembered you loved the Colonel's chicken." Then she yelled, "David, where are you, man, look who's here," and before it was out of her mouth he was standing in the doorway, grinning stupidly amid the haggard flabby skin on his face and the matted waves of dark hair on his head, and at almost the same instant I caught the smell of marijuana which had come in with him. Marie smelled it, too, because her face fell right down to her chest and her eyes showed anger, over it being so early in the day, I suppose.

But all of that was lost in David's booming talk. He snapped to attention and saluted me and he said, "By God, it's him, all dolled up like a general and covered in a hero's medals and looking like he could whip Cassius Clay with one arm tied behind his back." At first I thought he was mocking me — there was something in the tone of his voice — but then it changed and he was on me, shaking my hand and slapping my back in a big way as if we'd been best of friends all our lives. He gave me a bear hug and a "Whoopee!" and the dog hefted up to put in his two bits, barking and rubbing up against David and me, and there was the feeling of warm and friendly mayhem in a warm and friendly place. Marie was grinning at David by then. She shook her head in that manner women have which says I love you in spite of yourself, and I could see that she was hoping we'd hit it off together again.

David said, "You didn't tell him the surprise, did you?"

"No, I certainly did not," Marie said and she gave me a we've-got-a-secret look. She was about to go on with something when David interrupted too loudly with a "sit down here and take a load off and eat some of this good food," and Marie had to step in again, saying I might like to clean up first and relax.

"Why sure," he said, swaying a bit and holding on to the table for support. Then he sat down at the table and just stared at me with that stoned grin. So Marie showed me to Crissy's room and told me to make myself comfortable as Crissy would be sleeping with them for a while.

"Consider it yours till you get on your feet," she said.

It was a narrow bed, a kid's bed, but it was soft and folded around me like no military cot had ever done, and I intended to rest there for just a moment. Well, the next thing I knew David was standing over me, blocking the ceiling light, barking wake-up slogans like a drill sergeant, and when I dragged myself up I could tell it was quite dark outside.

~

We ate cold chicken and sent it down with two six packs of Dos Equis in the heavy brown bottles which they kept raising high to toast my return to the world. Then David rolled a number from what he called his "special reserve." By the time the dishes were in the sink we were all smiling and laughing, telling tales on each other, and then little Crissy started wanting to know when we were going to go see the surprise for Uncle John.

So David said, "Well, how about right now."

The four of us squeezed into the truck and David drove us back through town to the highway where we headed north. When I saw the eerie blue lights of the Alpine Regional Airport it came to me what the surprise was.

"Isn't she a sight," David said as the headlights lit up the plane, an old four-place job with the wings below the cockpit. It looked pretty scraped up. The windshield was cracked and one of the tie-downs was kicking in the breeze. "I call her Easy Rider," David said with a smile.

I asked him how he had come to own it and his smile really bloomed then: "Swapped for some work time and a little cash." To which Marie added, "A little cash, my foot, it was everything we'd put away," and I could tell this was still a sore point between them. When I asked how it handled, they were silent for a long time until Crissy mumbled, "It gots to be fixed."

Then David threw in, "That's what I've been wanting to talk to you about, Johnny." And all at once they were after me, telling me how this was our ticket to a future. If the plane were running, they said, David knew he could eventually set up enough commuter and cargo business that within a few years we could be working several planes between Alpine and El Paso and a number of points in between. They mentioned a dozen grand ideas. "And here's the mondo banana," David said. "Mexico! There's the real money. I'm talking the future now, once you've learned to fly."

"How much would it take?" I asked and they went silent again, glancing at each other, till David said, "Twelve-hundred."

"But I've only got a thousand."

"I can get the rest, no problem."

"That money's all I've got in the world, David."

"Make it nine-hundred then, and I promise I'll have it back to you within a month, and with plenty of interest to boot."

The feeling in the close confines of the truck cab at that moment was that there was much more to it than I'd been told. And I wasn't positive I was going to stay in Alpine even for a month. There was always Houston where I still had friends. But here were their hopeful faces, staring at me in the back glow of the headlights, and little Crissy sitting on my lap.

Marie said, "You don't have to, now, Johnny."

"That's right," said David. "There's no pressure being applied here. You do what you got to do."

But here were their faces, tired out from work and worry and hard living, and the buzz was wearing off for all of us.

Crissy put her head against my chest and I could feel her little body breathing, hear the faint wheeze in her lungs. I said, "Well, why not," and their eyes shone with relief and joy, and there was lots of expensive talk out of David on the way home.

II

So Alpine became my new address and I more or less settled in. I bought clothes and a clock radio and even began to scout around for a place to live once we got the business going.

David was in and out over the next few weeks as he scrambled for engine parts and the best deals on labor for the work he couldn't do himself. I occupied my time with repairing the motorcycle, which had been thrown in as part of the payback for my 900 dollars, and we went drinking in the bars at night after Crissy had been put to bed. I would pester David about his progress with the plane and he usually muttered something about a hydraulic valve or the carburetor and he would go on to other topics, vague things about the bright outlook for our lives. It was funny, we never talked about the war, other than to mention the places we had been and how glad we were that it was over for us. And even with just that little bit Marie would say, "That's enough now, let's talk about something else."

Then the big day came. I had gone up into the mountains on the motorcycle that afternoon, just to see them again and to think. It was dark when I got home, but the house was all lit up and in a real stir. Marie jumped on me immediately, wanting to know where I'd been, telling me that David had flown the plane.

"It's fixed," she said.

Then she disappeared into the back of the house. The smell of Mentholatum was heavy in the air and I could see the vaporizer spewing out mist back in their bedroom. Which meant Crissy'd had one of her attacks. Shepherd Fred wandered out to greet me and his old cloudy eyes seemed to be asking for help. Marie said David was waiting for me at the airport. When I asked about Crissy she glared at me as if I were the cause of her problems.

"She needs to go to the hospital, but we don't have the money, of course, and no insurance, of course, and the doctor won't speak to us anymore because we owe him so much — " She caught herself, let out a breath full of weariness. "Go on down there and take your ride and for God's sake be careful."

The plane was ready to go when I arrived, and it was making quite a racket. In the cockpit we could communicate only by yelling and pointing with our hands. All the seats were missing except the pilot's, so I had to sit on a crate and just hang on as best I could.

It was a beautiful sight once we crested the hills and David turned us south away from the town. A crescent of purple sunset was still glowing above the western horizon and the desert was a dark, ragged carpet below us. Soon David tapped my arm and hollered, "Spicville," pointing straight ahead, his face and hand shining green in the lights of the control panel. He banked it hard around to the north and took us home to a rough landing; we bounced and I heard scraping sounds behind me. David said there was plenty of work left to do, but the engine was sound and the plane solid enough to start earning a return on our investment.

"If we play it right," he said in the bar where we had gone to celebrate, "if we play it right, and act quickly, we could make enough *next week* to set us up for a long time to come."

I asked him what he meant and he looked at me across

the table with the face of a man who is still trying to decide something. He said, "Smuggling," and then he pulled back from the table, sitting up straight and proper as if to distance himself from the word. In a whisper he told me he had been in touch with a rancher up in the mountains who had fallen on hard times and was looking for a way to save his spread. The rancher had made contact with some business associates in Mexico.

"To put it simply," he said, "I'm talking a dope deal."

"Has this been your plan all along?" I asked and he nodded yes. "You mean I've already invested in a smuggling operation?"

He said, "Now listen, Johnny, like the old saying goes, it takes money to make money, and how the hell else would we get started? This is my chance, man. Let's face it, the only thing in my life that I've ever done right is fly airplanes. One deal like this is all we need.

"And there's another little item. Your sister's a wonderful woman. She took me out of the dirt and cleaned me off, and I've tried to take care of her because of it. But I'll tell you, unless something changes for us soon, I don't know how long we can last." He said, "And no telling what would happen then."

"You should have told me, David."

"Well, maybe I should have," he said. "But you never know about people, Johnny, how they've changed or whatever. I mean, I'm telling you all this on trust, you know. Nothing but trust."

Then we just sat there staring at the table until I asked him for more details. But he said no, he wasn't going to tell me any more, just in case. "Look, it's a good deal," he said. Most of it had been worked out, he told me, and there was very little risk: simply a matter of hopping down to a place in Mexico, hopping back to Alpine and then

waiting a few days to collect our share. He said, "If nothing else it's a way for you to help your sister and Crissy.
You could look at it that way, if you'd like."

"Does Marie know about this?" I asked.

"The question right now is you. Are you in?"

I told him that I'd have to think about it, to which he
said, "Fine. That's fine. But time is short." He seemed to
be watching me for something as if he were wondering
whether he should have told me about it, as if he wasn't
sure he trusted me now, now that I knew. "You'll keep it
quiet, of course," he said.

~

The house had calmed when we got home, but Crissy
was up all night coughing and wheezing, and in the morning she looked like she was close to death. Her skin had a
gray tint to it and her eyes were dark and frightened. She
needed help, Marie said. And I guess that's what made me
decide to do it. That, and, when I remember who I was
then, it was also the prospect of easy money and a
night's-worth of blind excitement.

When he told Marie she let loose with a fit, calling us
both losers and saying, "This is just what we need — both
of you in the penitentiary or dead somewhere in Mexico."
To me she said, "I thought you had more sense." They
argued for two days. He would leave, come back and leave
again. She talked about how after all those years of living
"low and fast" she thought she'd finally changed her life
into "something resembling normal," but now she saw that
people like her and David never really changed. "There is
in fact only one kind of life for each person in this world,"
she said. "There's respectable and nonrespectable and it's
just nonsense to think you can ever be anything else."

This kind of talk went on until I had almost changed

my mind. Then Crissy took a turn for the worse one night to the point that it sounded like she was drowning when she tried to catch her breath. We had to take her to the hospital. The doctor did something to her to make it better, but the hospital wouldn't let her stay even overnight, as she wasn't "serious" in their book and Marie and David were very far in arears on old bills.

In the truck, Marie said, "All right, do it. I guess you're going to whether I agree or not, and a mother with a sick child can't be choosy. But far as I'm concerned I know nothing about it. Do you hear me?" She let out a huff then and shoved Crissy onto my lap, like she was tired of the weight, and all the way home she was quiet, smoking cigarettes and staring out the window at something far away.

~

By now the outcome must appear obvious: that something went wrong with the scheme, that there was an accident or a double cross or that we got busted. But it was nothing like that, and this is the part I'm still trying to understand.

The night of the deal came and went just fine. We flew in the dark for about two hours, close above the hill tops, to what appeared to be a village. We landed on a road in the glare of headlights. Two men showed themselves. David spoke to them in Spanish. Then the four of us loaded half a dozen bales of marijuana into the plane. The smell was so strong that by the time we landed in a slight drizzle up in the mountains I had the feeling I'd been smoking the stuff steadily for a month or more.

It was an airstrip on a ranch. Again two men were waiting for us: the rancher and his son, about my age. We unloaded the bales into a pickup, covered it all with a tarp, and then David and I flew away into the mist. The only problem occurred back at Alpine Regional. David overshot the runway and the landing gears stuck in the mud as hard as if it were plaster of paris holding down the plane. He screamed at the plane and cursed and banged his fist against the controls until he sort of caught himself.

"David," I said but he just stared. "David!" I yelled and shook him and he came out of it, muttering, "They'll smell it. Anybody gets within fifty feet of this crate and they'll smell it." In the drizzle a man appeared from the control room, but I saw him in time and went over to him, convinced him we could take care of it. And we did. We hitched up a chain to the truck and freed the plane, then he taxied her very slowly to the farthest reaches of the field where we spent an hour cleaning it out.

At home Marie was in a state. The house was so full of her cigarette smoke that it was like stepping into a cloud. She said, "I don't want to hear a word about it," and then she closed herself up with Crissy back in their bedroom. David made himself a pallet of sleeping bags on the floor in my room. We all went to bed, but none of us slept that night. Marie was up and down. I heard her pawing through the icebox and muttering to old Shepherd Fred as if she were asking advice. In the glow of Crissy's night light I watched David's hands shake, saw his lips moving as he tried to moisten a parched mouth.

Outlaws we were not. But this is the part that baffled me, given what I knew about David and Marie, how long they had lived with uncertainty. The next morning and for days afterward as we waited for word from the rancher there was a kind of a sickness about the house. They hardly spoke to each other except to snap short responses to questions, and everybody's eyes were glassy from lack of sleep. David kept saying, "Something's gone wrong," and he drank a steady stream of beer and Old Crow as if it were medicine. Marie was so twisted up with fear that she called in to work and stayed home in bed, and she kept Crissy out of school. Whenever a car passed on the lonely dirt road out front David would leap up and peek out the window. He even talked to me of buying a pistol, but then he said, "It wouldn't do any good, I'd never use it." Smiling numbly at the floor, he said, "Maybe cyanide pills would be better, one for each of us."

Once, when we'd run out of food, and David and I tried to make a trip to the grocery store, he began to tremble so when we got into town that he had to pull off the road and let me drive. Over dinner that night he started talking about forgetting the whole deal, saying he'd been an idiot to think something like this would ever work for us and that because he was involved something was bound to go wrong. He called himself a "jinx on us." He said we should just pack up and move away, try to start out new. Which touched off Marie like I'd never seen before.

Holding a skillet in her hand she screamed at him for a fool and a coward, saying he'd put us all in jeopardy and now he'd just have to find the guts to go on with it. The sounds of mockery and challenge were in her voice.

"There's something wrong with you, David," she said. "You're lacking something that the rest of us have got — inside somewhere."

He sat there and took it, staring at the floor like he was being whipped, until finally he said, "I don't intend to ever see the inside of a prison again, for you or anybody else."

"I hope you're right," she said. "But it's a little late to be worrying about that. What are we supposed to live on, David?"

Just then, in that moment of silence, there came a knock on the front door. A ripple of panic moved over each of us. It might have been the sheriff for all we knew at that point. The faces above the table were ragged and blanched. Then David did something strange. It was something that, when I remember this — well, it was what changed everything; it made everything turn and veer off in a different direction. David's whole body was trembling when he leaned over and said gently, "Crissy, sweetheart, would you go see who it is and ask them to wait?"

Crissy gave him a sweet smile and started to leave, but Marie grabbed her by the shoulder and put her back in her chair.

"I'll get it," I said.

"No," said Marie. "David'll get it. Won't you, David?"

"Let him alone, Marie."

"Quiet," she said. "This has to do with more than just answering the door. This has to do with the past, doesn't it, David? This has to do with everything, doesn't it, David?"

"Shut up, Marie," he said softly, but she didn't listen.

"This has to do with sending other people to do your own nasty business, doesn't it, David? That you've been doing all your life and you're still trying to do it. Isn't that right, David?" She paused, breathing hard, and I watched him wither and writhe on his chair as she continued. "I may not be much to speak of, but I finish what I start and I don't send little girls, or young boys either for that matter — you know what I'm talking about, David? — I don't send other people to do what I ought to do myself so as to put them in danger. And I'm just a woman." She snorted a mean laugh then, the kind of laugh you hate to hear in a woman who's your sister. "Come on, David."

"Let it go, Marie," I said.

"No, it's too late for that. We can't let it go anymore."

The knock came again.

"Get up, David," she said. "Or I'll leave this house right now and you'll never see me again as long as you live."

At that she fell into her chair and stared at him like she was trying to force him to look up and meet her eyes.

"Do you hear me, David?"

David lifted his heavy body. There was something fierce but weary-looking about his face. For a moment he just stood there, straddling the chair, gazing at the top of the table. And all of a sudden he marched out of the kitchen. We heard his footsteps on the floor of the living room and then the front door opened. He returned in less than a minute, a good sign. Glancing at me, he nodded once and then moved around the kitchen in a panicky haste. He tossed down his beer and chased it with a gulp of Old Crow and then opened another beer. He said, "Don't leave the house," and he started out again. Marie called to him to wait a minute, but I told her to shut up and be still and I got up to follow him. In the dark living room he stopped me. He said he'd changed his mind and that I should stay with Marie and Crissy. He said he'd be back inside of three hours. He said, "Take care — " Then he smiled at me oddly like he wanted to mention something else but it wouldn't gel in his mind. So he shook my hand, once, firmly, and he was out the door before I could speak or move.

～

That was the last time I saw the man I call David Smith. And to this day I don't know exactly what happened up there in the mountains when he went to collect our share. What I remember of that night is how long it was, and quiet, and still — the sort of quiet, the sort of stillness you associate with a vigil — and how cold it was in the house.

We waited for him all through the wee hours. Then about sun-up a truck pulled into the yard. I peeked out the window, hoping, but it turned out to be the rancher's son standing on the porch. He looked awful. His freckled face was frightened and tired and dirty under his dirty cowboy hat. I stepped out and followed him to his truck where two canvas tote bags were waiting for me. He said, "I'm awful sorry about this, mister." When he looked up I knew. From his eyes, I suppose. There was something missing in them, like the eyes of men I'd seen in the war.

"There was a crash," he said. "We don't know what went wrong. The weather was clear, the plane sounded fine. But soon as he cleared the ground that old rig went right for this hill up there."

He kept glancing around as he talked, as if something huge and horrible were lurking in the desert. It was quite a risk, his coming back down there to bring us what was ours. None of this was a part of the plan and he had his own problems now and he wanted to be gone from there as soon as possible.

"Right before he took off he must have heaved these two sacks out the window. That's how he'd asked for it: 'Split up the money two ways,' he told us. There's enough in there for you and your sister to get away and start out new somewheres. That's what I'd suggest. And you better hurry. We all better hurry."

The rancher's son got in his truck then and drove off into the pretty sunrise as I turned for the house, thinking of Marie and Crissy, and trying to figure how I was going to say it to her, how I would have to state the simple facts coldly and call it an accident. I thought about the trouble we were in. I thought about running. There was Marie on the porch in her robe and furry slippers, a cigarette in her mouth, her arms holding herself just below her breasts. At that moment she looked weathered and worn out, like some old gal you might find behind the counter of an all-night truck stop in a worthless town such as Gallup, New Mexico. She said, "It's all over, isn't it."

III

Shame, in my book, works like this. Once you've done a rotten thing, once you've turned on somebody that once was yours, once you've let good sense or courage or whatever push loyalty to some deep dungeon in your gut, some place that you'll never find it again — well, once you've done this you've set yourself a new path in life and you have no choice but to go on down it.

By the time we settled everything that day, packed what was necessary, retrieved the truck from the airport and got out of town on a back road, it was late afternoon. At Van Horn, a dusty little stop up on I-10, we took a room at an old motor court called The Sands. Back of the motel was a weedy lot where we parked the truck and the cycle so they couldn't be seen, and then I walked up Business 10 to a Church's Chicken place and brought home supper. After we ate, Marie put Crissy to bed and then the dog let it be known that he needed a walk to relieve himself. Marie followed me when I went out with him and in the lot behind the motel we sat on the tailgate of the truck while the dog was searching around for a place to make his mark. Marie hadn't opened her mouth for hours, but suddenly she said, "You know what I wish?" and I looked at her, ready to listen.

"This has been on my mind all day for some reason," she said. She pulled up her sweater against the night air and she looked at the starry sky and she seemed almost to be reading something up there, she paused so long. Then she said, "I wish I owned a pair of white sandals, with little straps across the back and with low, pointed heels. Like some I saw on a woman once."

"At this time of year?" I said and she smiled at me shyly.

"And I wish I had a little white dress with one tiny rose embroidered right over my breast here." She gently touched her breast as if imagining what the rose would feel like. "I wish it was summertime and that I was in the Rocky Mountains of Canada, at some lodge or resort. My only thought would be what to eat for supper and then whether to go dancing or sightseeing or just go to bed in the nice clean sheets."

She said, "You've never been to Canada, have you."

I told her no, though I've been there since.

"It's real pretty country," she said. "Nothing like this around here. I went once with a man I knew. A pilot, of course. Sort of a vacation. This was before I met David and I left Crissy with some people in Corpus, good people that would baby-sit for me. They were neighbors of mine who went to church and everything, and they would take Crissy with them, and they were always after me to go too. Can you imagine that? Me in church?"

I said, "Yes, I can imagine that," which caused her to smile and to look at me as if I were too naive to understand anything.

"Anyway," she said, "we stayed at a place on Lake Louise, and for two weeks we did nothing but play and make love. He was a nice man, as I remember, even though it didn't work out for us. Nothing ever works out, I guess. But for two weeks it was good and fun, and I thought maybe I was in love with the man. For a while I thought about not coming home at all. I thought about just living there with him and leaving Crissy with those people." She said, "That's awful, isn't it, to think such a thing?"

I said something about it depending on circumstances, but she wasn't listening. She said, "There were even times when she was a baby that I actually thought of leaving her on somebody's doorstep, figuring she'd be better off with anybody but me. There were times when I thought about just getting rid of her."

Shepherd Fred had returned by now and he was sitting at our feet grinning up at us. It was perhaps nine o'clock. I was starting to think again about what was up ahead, about what it meant to be on the run and that we would have to find a newspaper in the morning to see if there was a report on us, and that we would have to decide what to do if there was, or even if there wasn't. This was my family, what was left of it, and I wanted to do my best by them. I wanted to talk to Marie about it, though I knew she was still in shock, as she had a certain wisdom in such matters and since I was thinking I wanted us to face it together.

"Listen, Marie," I began, but she interrupted me.

"No, don't," she said. "I'd appreciate it if you wouldn't. I suppose you think I'm a pretty worthless human being, don't you, after what I did to David. And maybe it would be better just not to talk about it. Most worthless things are better left alone."

"I don't think any such thing, Marie."

"Well, I do. What I did was a rotten thing, as rotten as it gets. It was not something a woman should ever do to a man she loves. And I want you to know I'll never do it again."

The dog made a whining sound at that moment and Marie looked at him with affection. She reached down and scratched his ears and he thumped his tail in appreciation, staring up at her as if she were the center of the universe. "Do whatever you think is best, Johnny," she said, giving me a look direct as any I've ever seen. When she seemed satisfied with what she saw, she told the dog to come and together they went off slowly to the room, leaving me there to think.

After a while, once I'd sorted it out as best I could, I went into the room myself. Before sleep came, as I lay exhausted under my covers, I could hear Marie humming some tune and hear her muttering the words — a lullaby or a hymn perhaps. She was sitting on their bed, sort of petting Crissy and old Fred, first one then the other, looking down at them both as they slept, sweet as anything. I don't know how long this went on, or whether she slept at all, because in the morning Marie wasn't around to talk about it. The motorcycle was missing and she had put all but a couple hundred dollars of our take into my bag before she left. I should have seen this coming, but a mind can take in only so much and mine was worn out with worry. It was many years before I got rid of the worry, and even today there remains a lingering feel of it in my blood. I haven't seen my sister, the woman I call Marie Smith, since that night, in that cheap motel room, with the neon light of the sign out front glowing through the window curtain. It's an image of her that has always stayed with me: Marie on the bed, bent over, humming to herself, touching her loved ones for the last time.